Scarsdale
Crematorium

The Haunted Series
Book 4
Patrick Logan

Books by Patrick Logan

The Haunted Series
Book 1: Shallow Graves
Book 2: The Seventh Ward
Book 3: Seaforth Prison
Book 4: Scarsdale Crematorium

Insatiable Series
Book 1: Skin
Book 2: Crackers
Book 3: Flesh
Book 4: Parasite
Book 5: Stitches (Spring 2017)

Family Values Trilogy
Witch (Prequel)
Mother
Father
Daughter (Spring 2017)

Short Stories
System Update

Prologue

THE ONLY SOUNDS THAT could be heard in the helicopter were the chuffing of the blades and the rain pelting on the windows.

But other than that, not one of the passengers said a word.

Robert's eyes were downcast, his gaze locked on his blood-covered hands. They were trembling.

He had taken a man's life today, a man that had been alive. This wasn't like James Harlop or George Mansfield or even Andrew Shaw.

This was different.

Father Callahan had been a living, breathing human being, and although his body had been torn in half and he'd been well on his way to death, Robert had pushed him over the brink. He had killed him—mercifully, certainly, but his actions weren't without repercussions.

And that said nothing of what Sean had done: killing the man with the bound hands, shoving the warden into the Marrow.

Robert interlaced his fingers, trying to force them to stop shaking.

"So," Cal said at long last, breaking the silence. Robert lifted his eyes, a process that was strangely laborious.

He was exhausted—mentally and physically spent.

Cal wasn't addressing him; instead, he was looking at the boy in the round glasses, his eyes bulging from behind the thick lenses that were streaked with blood.

"So, you want to be a ghostbuster, do ya?"

Allan Knox didn't respond. Instead, his hands continued to fiddle with the shattered remnants of a camera that rested on his lap. Instead of answering, the man — more a boy than a man, really, although it was clear that he had aged considerably this day — removed the oddly undamaged red lens from the camera body. He wiped some blood from the red lens, then held it up to one eye and stared through it at Cal.

What he said next surprised all of them.

"Yes," he said, his voice dry and hoarse. He cleared his throat before continuing. "Yes, this is what I always wanted."

Robert stared at Allan, his mouth twisting into a grimace. He bit his tongue, a scathing remark hiding just behind his teeth.

How could you want this? This...this death...death everywhere. How can anyone want this?

Robert wished more than anything that he had never become immersed in this world. Even though Shelly had scolded him for the words, when he had uttered them back then, he had done so partially in jest. This time, however, Robert really wished that he had been in the car with his family when they'd died.

When Amy had died...

Amy...how is Amy involved in all of this? Why is she involved?

So many questions rattled around in his skull that it made his head spin. He had gone into the fiasco thinking that he might get some answers out of it, but, if anything, his time at Seaforth had only made things more confusing.

Carson...

"ETA eleven minutes to the estate," the pilot's voice crackled in his headset.

And the book — Inter vivos et mortuos — what was in the book that Father Callahan wanted me to see? That he would waste his final words on telling me to get it? Was it about Amy? The prophecy?

"Got it," Sean answered.

Robert shook his head.

The book...I need to find the book. It has to have answers in it.

"No," he croaked.

Everyone in the helicopter turned to look at him: Sean, Shelly, Allan, Cal. Even Aiden in the copilot's seat whipped his head around.

He wasn't sure if they were more shocked by what he had said, or by the simple fact that he had spoken.

Robert turned his gaze to the window, a deliberate effort to make sure that he wasn't convinced otherwise by Shelly or Cal after he said what he was going to next.

"I'm not going to the estate," he said simply.

"What? Robert—" Shelly leaned toward him as she spoke, but Robert just closed his eyes and shook his head. After a deep breath, he opened them again and mustered the courage to look at her.

Shelly had since leaned back in her chair, arms folded across her ample chest. Yet despite her frustrated posture, her expression didn't match.

Her features were painted in sheer sadness.

"I can't go back," he nearly whispered, once again averting his gaze. "There is something else I need to do."

Part I - Camera Tricks

THREE MONTHS LATER

Chapter 1

JONAH SILVERS GRUNTED AND wiped his forehead with the back of his gloved hand. The glove was black with soot, serving only to spread the grime around rather than removing it.

He spat on the concrete floor before turning back to the oven and peering inside.

"Fuck," he muttered, shaking his head. He had turned the burners off too soon, again. Wiping sweat from his eyes, he could see that not all the bones had been rendered into dust; he could still clearly make out the skull, the hip bones, even an outline of a spinal cord covered in black soot.

Jonah glanced around as he weighed his options. It would take another thirty minutes or so just to get the oven up to temp, and now that what was left of the body had cooled, it would take at least another hour before they would be reduced to dust.

His eyes eventually wandered until they fell on the body bag that he had opened right before he had switched off the oven. The woman's face stared out at him with cold, dead eyes. He had pulled the thick plastic bag down to her navel, revealing large, white breasts.

"It's your fault, Mrs. Kyra," he said, then stifled a giggle. His eyes remained locked on the woman's pale breasts, and it took all of his willpower to look back to the oven.

There was more than just Mrs. Kyra to get to today; there were three more bodies to be burned, and it was already closing in on midnight.

Jonah made up his mind, and pushed the shovel forward. Then, with sweat pouring from his face from the heat still radiating from the oven, he used the corner to shove the skull to the very back. He did the same with the hip bones. Thankfully, what he had thought was a spinal cord ended up being just air pockets left behind from the old bones. Jonah scooped a shovelful of soot, and poured it into the plastic lined box at his feet. Dust puffed up and clung to the exposed areas on his face, wrists, and neck that were slick with sweat.

Jonah barely noticed.

After several more shovelfuls, he turned his attention to the bag, eying the gray powder inside the dark bag.

It's enough, he surmised. *Shit, I doubt anyone even looks in these things.*

Satisfied with his work, Jonah leaned down then lifted the box and slammed it on the table behind him with the three others. Then he turned back to Mrs. Kyra.

Jonah tilted his head to one side, inspecting the woman again. Her eyes were sunken, her cheeks sallow. The makeup that they had used for the open casket had either been wiped away, or her present state of decay had limited its effectiveness.

Still...she didn't look half bad for a fifty-three-year-old dead schoolteacher.

"Aw, it's too bad we don't have more time to play, hon. Would love to teach you some things...some things that I didn't learn in school."

Jonah snorted as he bent to pick her up, giving her left breast one final hard squeeze. Seeing his finger marks remain on her pale flesh, which didn't return to its original shape, brought about another chuckle.

Then he got to business, hoisting her body onto his left shoulder with a grunt. She was heavier than he had thought, and Jonah needed to force his considerable gut backwards to make sure he didn't topple forward under her weight. At a mere five foot three, Jonah was glad that his build—thick, over-weight—kept his center of gravity low, rooted.

Dropping Mrs. Kyra's body onto the table beside the cre-mated remains, he began the process of taking her out of the bag. Sure, it would have been easier to do this on the ground, but it was dark in the basement, and he wanted to get a good look at her. Jonah slipped her feet out of the body bag first, of-fering a long, lingering look at the mound of pubic hair between her legs. He cursed himself at not planning his time right, be-fore he pulled her all the way out of the bag and put her on his shoulder again.

Jonah pivoted, and dropped the body onto the lip of the oven. He had intended on putting her on her ass first, then low-ering the top half of her body, but Mrs. Kyra had some meat to her ass and thighs, and he again underestimated her weight—and her state of rigor.

The body fell backwards, and for a brief moment Jonah tried his best to hold her upright. But it was a losing battle, and what did it really matter, anyway? Mrs. Kyra was dead.

Jonah stepped away from the oven and watched as her body fell, her head cracking loudly off the ceramic tiles. Her body even bounced a little before coming to a complete rest.

Placing his palms against the soles of her feet, this time pre-pared for her weight, he leaned in and shoved hard. A horrible scraping sound—toughened, leather-like skin passing over the remaining bone fragments—echoed inside the oven, but Jonah paid this no heed.

He had heard it before—many times.

After a final heave, he headed around the side of the large oven, which he sometimes joked would make the world's fastest pizza, and then hammered the big red button with a filthy glove-covered palm. There was a throaty rumble from somewhere below his feet, followed by the hiss of gas being released. Jonah quickly walked to the front again, eager to watch the body burn.

This was his favorite part—watching as the flames first licked at the underside of the bodies, causing the skin to bubble and then turn black. The smell was bad, even he recognized that, but he was so lost in a euphoric state as the hair burned, the eyes sizzled and popped, the breasts deflated, that he barely noticed.

And deep underground in the basement of the Scarsdale Crematorium, Jonah was free to watch at his leisure. It was times like these that he relished.

The first of the flames shot up from the grates below, sending a roaring heat that splashed his face, illuminating his wide nose and soot-smeared features in an orange glow.

His lips parted in a sneer, and he could feel the front of his pants, covered in a thick, heavy apron, start to tighten.

Some days, if he was lucky, the flames would cause the body to sit upright. It was rare, but it did happen.

Jonah knew he should be putting the other remains away, fill out the stupid completion log that his asshole boss made him do each time, and that he was already behind schedule, but he just had to watch.

Just for a little while.

Just until Mrs. Kyra was no longer recognizable.

And then, to his absolute delight, as the flames continued to blacken and crisp the underside of her body, Mrs. Kyra started to rise.

Jonah clapped his hands together in glee, the tightness in the front of his pants growing to such an extent that it made it nearly impossible to stand upright without causing him discomfort.

The oven was more than ten feet deep and four feet wide, but it wasn't very tall—at only three feet high, when Mrs. Kyra's body started to bend at the waist, it could only make it to a third of the way to a sitting position before her head, eyes still blank, cloudy orbs, *thunked* against the top. There was a sizzle as the skin on her forehead bound to the hot ceramic.

"It's a good day," he whispered to himself, his eyes twinkling as they reflected the flames. "A real good day."

He had been working at the crematorium for more than three years now, and had cremated hundreds of bodies in that time, but this was only the fourth time that a body had sat up like this.

The first time it had happened, Jonah had nearly lost his shit. And that time—that one time—he had been glad that Vinny had been there with him.

"Happens sometimes," the man had told him in his dopey, nasally voice. "Dunno why, and it's freaky as hell, but it happens. That's why I put the screen up."

But Jonah hated the screen—a mesh-like door designed to keep the heat in, but one that also blocked his view.

Now, on this fourth occasion, the body sitting up had a completely different effect on him.

Case in point: the tightness in his jeans.

He lived for this shit—who would have thought that dropping out of high school after being bullied ad nauseam for years would have landed him here? There was no way that even the shithole that was Scarsdale should have hired him given his history.

But they had, and now he was here.

And he fucking loved it.

It was his calling, that much was obvious. It made him wonder why his guidance counselor had suggested a plumbing apprenticeship, of all things.

Fuck that.

As Jonah watched, Mrs. Kyra—which incidentally wasn't her real name; every woman in the crematorium was named after his high school teacher, the one that had scolded, then touched him—continued to rise with unusual determination. Her forehead continued to push into the ceiling of the oven, forcing her neck forward.

"Oh, this is a very good day," he said with a giggle. In fact, it was so good that he reached around his neck and slipped the apron off, letting it drop to the floor in a heap. Then he grabbed his erection through his jeans, squeezing it hard with the filthy glove.

As he watched, fixated by a mixture of pleasure and disgust, the flames continued to burn her lower half, causing her legs to blacken to a crisp. But because she was sitting up, her top half, including her pasty white breasts, was relatively unscathed. Protocol was to force her back down again using the shovel, at least that was what Vinny did, but there was no way that he was going to do that. In fact, the way she was sitting up…if her lower half weren't so charred, he would have considered taking her out again and having his way with her.

Mrs. Kyra continued to sit up, the pressure on her forehead such that it was causing her throat to bulge out like a goiter. And yet the pressure seemed to be increasing instead of subsiding.

The other three bodies that had sat up had slowly lowered again as the temperature inside the oven reached a certain threshold. But this…this Mrs. Kyra seemed to be sitting up even harder as the temperature rose.

"Yeah, a very, very—"

But something happened, something so unexpected that even Jonah was at a loss for words.

The pressure was too much for Mrs. Kyra's tight, dead flesh, and her throat suddenly split, a surprisingly clean and bloodless gash that caused her head to flop backward, revealing the inside of her throat.

"Wow," he whispered, momentarily pausing his rhythmic grasping of his erection.

This was new. And new was exciting.

But what happened next made Jonah immediately soft. The two halves of her neck started to move, like a giant, lipless mouth. And then, as he swallowed hard, he thought that the movements started to look less random, as if trying to form words.

And then, to his utter horror, he heard a voice.

"Jonaaaaaaaaaaaaaah."

"Wh—wh—wh—wh—?" Jonah blubbered. He stumbled backward, but his progress was halted by the table with the bags of ashes on them.

"Jonaaaaaaaaaah," that lipless gash hissed just loud enough to be heard over the sound of the roaring flames. "Come join me in here, Jonaaaaaaaaaaaah."

"Wha—what the fuck is going on?" he stammered.

This was new, but it wasn't so exciting anymore; instead, it was downright terrifying.

Jonah crouched down, his eyes still locked on Mrs. Kyra's neck wound, and grabbed the shovel in his right hand, before rising to his feet again.

"Jonaaaaaah, it's nice and cozy in here. Why don't you join me?"

Jonah swallowed hard and gripped the shovel even tighter. And then, inexplicably, he took a step forward.

"Yes, that's right, Jonah, join Mrs. Kyra…join meeeeeeeeee!"

"No," he whispered, but his actions belied his words. He took another step forward, then another. And then he dropped the shovel, which clanged loudly on the cement floor.

The last thing Jonah Silvers wanted to do was to move closer to the oven, with or without Mrs. Kyra speaking to him. The heat alone was unbearable.

And yet he continued to slide forward. It was as if this woman, the one with the breasts that were still deformed from his squeezing, had some sort of hold on him.

"Yes," the neck exclaimed, before breaking into a long, slow laugh. "Yes, Jonah, yes."

Jonah's vision started to darken, the bright orange and yellow flames seeming to dim despite him being closer now. And then, when he was within two feet of the oven, the heat so powerful that he felt his lips start to blister, Jonah did the unthinkable.

He reached out and put both of his hands on the scalding ledge of the oven. Even through the heavy gloves, there was an immediate hiss of his flesh searing, but he took no notice.

All Jonah wanted to do was to crawl inside the oven—to cuddle up next to Mrs. Kyra, to give her tit one final squeeze.

And he would have. There was no doubt in his twisted mind that that was exactly what he would have done.

But a voice, another voice, drew him back.

"Get over here, Jonah."

Jonah turned his head around, and this broke whatever spell the corpse had on him.

There was a man in the shadows, a tall, thin man that was but a silhouette in the darkness. Jonah tried to pull away, intending on grabbing the shovel, but his gloves had bonded to the hot ceramic.

"Vinny?" he asked, pain starting to shoot up his arms. "Vinny, is that you? I need—I need help, please, Mrs. Kyra— Mrs. Kyra, she—"

The silhouette shook his head.

"It's not Vinny—but I've seen what you've done here."

Jonah suddenly gritted his teeth. He was immediately transported back to the time when Johnny Parker had peered over the top of the stall and had caught him masturbating in the ninth grade. That single act had set his life careening into a downward spiral of torment and self-loathing. That was why he liked his job so much—the dead never complained. The dead never mocked or teased him.

"You've seen nothing! I was doing nothing! Just my job, that's all!" he yelled.

The man in the shadows laughed, and Jonah's fury grew. With newfound strength, he managed to peel his hands away from the ceramic oven, leaving two rubber handprints and several layers of bubbling skin behind.

Still, he barely acknowledged the horrible pain that shot up his arms.

"You laugh at me?" he hissed. "You dare laugh at Jonah Silvers? Do you know who I am? Do you know what I've done?"

Jonah's eyes darted to the shovel that he had dropped earlier. He didn't know if he would be able to grip it with his mangled hands, but he was determined to try.

"You saw nothing!" he screamed. "I'll fucking kill you!"

But the man's laughter only increased in pitch.

"Oh, Jonah, you couldn't kill me. You can't do anything to me. In fact, you're just a little fucking pervert, aren't you? Diddling dead bodies—that's your thing, isn't it? It's not killing."

Jonah's rage abated, as it had that day more than twenty years ago. It fled him because the man was right. He was no killer. He never was. He was just a weak, pathetic pervert.

"You know what I like about you, Jonah? I like that you're loyal, and that's what I need right now. Someone who is loyal."

"What—what do you need me for?" Jonah asked, his voice meek now.

"I'm building an army."

"An army? What—?"

But then the man stepped forward, and for the first time since he had appeared, seemingly out of midair, he stepped into the light from the fire.

A gasp escaped Jonah as the man laid a gentle hand on his shoulder.

"Carson? Is that you? How—?"

But then the man started laughing again, cutting off his words.

Chapter 2

"YOU HAVE THE CAMERA set up?"

Allan double-checked the lens, making sure that it was screwed on tight.

"Yes?" Cal asked.

"Yep, we're good," he replied, trying to keep the trepidation he felt in his chest from leaking into his voice.

"You sure?"

Allan shrugged, his confidence eking out of him with every subsequent query.

"Think so, think so."

Shelly threw up her arms.

"This is fucking stupid. Really? Using the cameras to, what, capture the quiddity?"

Cal pulled his eye away from the camera and stared at Shelly over the smattering of tombstones.

"What, Shelly? What do you want us to say? What could we possibly say that would make you happy? Huh?"

Shelly stared back at him for a moment, then she crossed her arms over her chest and pursed her lips.

"Well?"

"Never mind."

She took a step backward, as if conceding her contribution to the half-cocked experiment.

But Cal wasn't done—not yet. Ever since Robert had forced Sean to lower the helicopter in an empty field, of all places, and had gotten out despite his, Shelly's, and Sean's pleas, she had been acting off.

And that was three months ago.

Fuck her. Like Rob, it isn't always about you, Shelly. Get over yourself.

"He's not coming back, Shel. Just accept that, move on. I have. He's a selfish prick, left us here to deal with this mess all by ourselves."

Shelly's face scrunched, and for a brief moment, he thought he had pushed her beyond the breaking point.

Tough love—she needs tough love.

But then, to his surprise, her expression relaxed.

"You're right, Cal. I'm sorry."

The response was so foreign that it floored him, and he immediately changed his tone.

"Guys? I think we should pay attention. I mean, I get that—"

"Shel? You okay? You want to—?"

"Guys!"

The fear in Allan's voice drew Cal's gaze away from Shelly's downcast eyes.

"What, Allan? What is it?"

He hadn't intended for the words to come out with such vehemence, but the truth was that he shared some of Shelly's apprehension about the whole setup.

It was Allan who had proposed the idea, which came as no surprise, as he was the only one of the three who had any savvy when it came to computers or technology. He said he had been working on an idea, an idea that the cameras that he had fashioned that could see the quiddity might also be able to capture them.

It sounded farfetched, but what was he supposed to do? Cal didn't even consider doing what Robert had back in Seaforth: demanding the quiddity to stop. He had no fucking clue how Robbo had done that—none of them did—or even exactly *what* he had done, but it was clear to them that it was something that was unique to him.

"Guys? There's someone here."

Cal snapped out of his head and looked up from the one of three cameras that they had set up to triangulate the quiddity.

A tall, thin man with thick gray hair stepped into the clearing. Cal gaped and stared at the man, who seemed, at least for the moment, oblivious to their presence.

Well, no matter how farfetched, we are going to put it to the test sooner rather than later.

The man's eyesight must have been poor; he moved cautiously through the tall grass at a snail's pace. Cal had had a blind aunt once, and she'd walked the same way, the soles of her feet always staying in contact with the ground to ensure that there were no surprise stairs or cliffs looming.

Cal looked to Shelly, who was staring bug-eyed at the man, who he realized was dressed in some sort of naval regalia. She must have sensed his gaze, because she slowly turned her head to face him. Cal shrugged, then indicated the camera mounted on a tripod a few feet from her.

Shelly slid toward the camera.

"Hello? Who's there?" the man suddenly shouted, lifting his head. Cal turned to Allan next, mouthing the words, 'What the fuck do we do now?'

Allan used his finger to indicate the area in the grass that they had aimed the only light at, where they planned to lure the quiddity into in order to test the boy's insane theory.

How the fuck am I supposed to get him to walk through there?

The man with the gray hair suddenly turned his nose skyward and appeared to be sniffing the air.

"I know you bastards are here," he spat. "What have you done with my wife?"

Cal shook his head.

His wife?

The man's confused demeanor reminded him of the guard at Seaforth, and before that, Jacky Harlop, desperately cleaning the floor of the Harlop Estate.

'Go!' Allan mouthed. 'Go!'

Cal took another look at the blind man sniffing the air, and decided what the hell. Being blind, or nearly blind, there was no way that the man would be able to catch him if things went wrong.

And maybe it was a good time to test his new energy and physique.

Cal made up his mind and stepped forward into the clearing between the whitewashed tombstones.

"Hey!" he shouted, giving a shrug to Shelly when she narrowed her eyes at him.

"I knew it," the man sneered. "Where is she?"

Cal took another step, making sure that the clearing was directly between himself and the old man.

"Yeah, we have your wife...why don't you come and get her?"

The man paused, still sniffing the air.

And then his old bones seemed to defrost, and he suddenly bolted, sprinting at an alarming speed toward Cal.

"Shit!" Cal yelled, his eyes bulging. He swiveled and started to run in the opposite direction as the old man quickly closed the twenty or so feet between them. His first instinct was to flee into the woods, to get the fuck away from the crazed navy officer who seemed to be channeling his inner Usain Bolt, but Allan's shout directed him elsewhere.

"Cal! The camera! Get to the camera!"

He took a hard right, skidding on the dewy grass. Breathing heavily, he righted himself behind the camera just as the man sped into the triangulated area.

"Now!" Allan shouted. "Take the picture now!"

Cal, red-faced, his legs burning, didn't even bother to look through the viewfinder. Instead, he just jammed the shutter button on top furiously.

But the man just kept coming.

"Allan?" he shouted.

But it was too late; the quiddity in the navy regalia crashed directly into his tripod.

And then he fell on top of Cal.

Chapter 3

"AND THE RIFT IS closed?"

Sean Sommers nodded.

"Closed," he confirmed. The figure sitting across from him was draped in a heavy cloak, blanketing his features in shadows. When he spoke, his words were constricted and androgynous.

"Did you do it?"

Sean shook his head.

"No? Who, then?"

"Robert," he said. "Robert took out the keeper of the book, closed the rift. Leland was still trapped inside."

The man in the cloak tilted his head slightly, as if contemplating Sean's words, and the hood shifted, revealing a pasty white chin. His hands, which were smaller than Sean might have thought given the man's raspy voice, quickly moved to pull it tight again.

"What about the book? Did you locate the book?"

Sean shook his head.

"Negative. Had some men check out the church, but they couldn't locate it. But...but I think you should know that we aren't the only ones looking for it."

Again, the head tilt.

"No?" the man asked, surprise on his tongue. "You did say that Carson died in the explosion — we went to great lengths to cover that up, Sean. It wasn't easy convincing the media that the explosion off the shore of New Jersey was from a gas bubble, unearthed by recent seismic activity. But those that knew of the prison...they were more difficult to persuade."

Sean again shook his head.

"No, Carson's dead."

There was a short pause.

"You're sure?"

Sean looked down at his hands when he answered.

"Yes. Did it myself," he lied. "Robert took out the priest, I took out Carson."

"And what of Robert now? Robert and his gang? Are they ready for their next task?"

Sean's fingers tensed on the hard wooden table.

"No, that's the thing...it's Robert who's looking for the book. He knows of the prophecy."

For a long time, the man across from him said nothing. Eventually, when the silence dragged on for so long that Sean started to feel as if time had slowed, as it had back at the prison, he raised his gaze.

"Sir? Is—?"

"How many Guardians are left, Sean?"

Sean did some mental math.

"Three," he said firmly.

"And the rift can only be opened using one of them—that's what the prophecy says, correct? A Guardian or the Keeper of the Book?"

Sean nodded.

"Yes—three, now that the Keeper is gone. Only a Guardian trapped between worlds can open the rift, and only the girl can hold it open long enough for the souls to come back."

The man in the cloak made a sucking sound with his teeth.

"Let me ask you something, Sean: what good are the Guardians if they can't guard anything? If their very existence threatens the solemnity of the Marrow?"

Sean bit his lip, knowing what was coming next.

"Wouldn't it be easier just to eliminate every one of them?"

Sean didn't answer. The cloaked man knew, of course, that Sean himself was one of the remaining three.

"For now, let's just keep it simple. Find the book, Sean—we wouldn't want it landing in the wrong hands. That's your priority. Are the others at the Harlop Estate still of use?"

Sean contemplated this for a moment. There was Shelly, of course, but the other two...

"Maybe," he said at last.

"Maybe," the man repeated. "Your ambivalence in this situation is alarming. After all, this is your mess—it was you who revealed yourself to Robert and brought him into the fold, which started this whole chain of events. You are aware of this, aren't you? I specifically recommended that you keep him out of this."

Again, Sean remained silent.

The man sighed.

"What are the chances that Robert finds the book?"

"Low—minimal. If my men couldn't find it, then I doubt he can. But, I feel compelled to tell you that the man's power is growing. He singlehandedly—"

The man waved his hand dismissively.

"You need to find the book. That is your priority. Even though the rift is closed for now, I still sense a disturbance. There are more dead hanging around than there should be. If the Harlop Trio are still of use, send them to vanquish some of the more aggressive ones. But find the book."

Sean nodded and started to stand, his hand sneaking into his pocket and fondling the worn package of cigarettes therein.

"But this time, Sean, be discreet about it. There will be no more accidents."

Sean swallowed hard and nodded briskly before leaving the room.

Once outside the apartment complex, he lit his cigarette and inhaled deeply.

There will be no more accidents.

Obtuse, vague.

Unfortunately, Sean was well aware of what would happen to him if he slipped up again.

Chapter 4

MICHAEL GRANT YOUNG TURNED off the shower and stepped onto the heated slate tiles. As the steam billowed around him, he grabbed one of several plush cotton towels with the initials MGY on the trim and wrapped it around his waist. Deliberately, but without haste, he walked to the mirror next, allowing time for the fog to clear.

As he continued to wait, Michael set up his shaving utensils: he laid the Silvertip Badger hair shaving brush on the Cesar stone countertop, then gently put the container of bespoke shaving cream, which had been specifically designed for his skin, beside it. The straight razor came next, but with this item Michael took an additional moment to confirm that it was still sharp, holding it up and angling it in the natural lighting. Satisfied, he placed that alongside the other accoutrements. When he raised his eyes, the fog had cleared.

In the mirror was the reflection of a well-groomed man in his late thirties, with short, jet-black hair, a strong jaw, perfectly straight nose, and eyes that matched his hair in intensity and color.

Handsome, by any standard.

But that was only his reflection; the real Michael Grant Young was buried deep inside, so deep that it would take much more than a mirror to reveal his true nature. And the true Michael Young was something far, far uglier. The image in the mirror was only the empty shell that housed his *self*, his uniqueness, his essence, which was far greater than the sum of meat and bones and organic matter.

And real; *that* Michael Young was the real Michael Young, the one that few got to see and lived to talk about it.

He smiled and picked up the brush, gently dipping the soft hair into the cream. He was about to bring it to his cheek when he noticed several streaks of blood just beneath his jaw line.

Smirking, he dampened a white washcloth, also monogrammed, and wiped the blood away. Then he set about lathering his face and completed the same shaving ritual he had performed for the last five years.

After shaving, Michael dressed in a bespoke navy suit, complete with a tie three shades lighter than the jacket. Using the long brass shoehorn hanging on the inside of his walk-in closet, Michael slid his tan loafers on.

Then he headed downstairs to the chef's kitchen.

He opened the stainless steel fridge door, and a coy smile crept onto his face as he surveyed the interior. It was nearly empty, a consequence of the intermittent fasting that he had been partaking in for years now. There were, however, several bottles of sparkling water lining the door, and he grabbed one. After closing the fridge, he leaned up against it, unscrewed the cap, and took a long swig. He swished the liquid around in his mouth and then swallowed.

The effervescent bubbles tickled his throat as they went down, and he waited for the sensation to hit his stomach before taking another big sip.

All told, Michael downed half the bottle before screwing the cap back on and putting it in the fridge with the others. A quick glance at his Rolex revealed that it was almost seven, which meant he was right on schedule.

He was halfway to the front door of his condo when a muted voice drifted up to him.

Michael frowned; the lower level was supposed to be soundproof—*had* been soundproof, until a few moments ago.

"Please..." the female voice whimpered. "Please let me go...I'll—I'll do anything."

It was difficult for him to make out the exact words as they filtered up through the furnace vent, or however they managed to find him, but he knew what they were nonetheless.

The women always said the same thing.

Michael rolled his eyes, and his hand slipped away from the doorknob. After short pause, he swiveled and briskly walked to the door beside the kitchen. He had had it covered in a thin veneer and painted to look exactly the same as the other doors in the house, but there was something about it that was just a little *off*. It was a consequence of being manufactured from three-inches of solid steel, he supposed.

A necessary evil, as it were.

With a sigh, Michael placed his thumb on the fingerprint reader off to the right, and then waited as the lock disengaged. When he opened the door, his nose crinkled at the smell of must and rot.

Unlike the pristine upper floor to his condo, the lower half— the one that had cost him a pretty penny to have constructed, given that they had to essentially build a basement from scratch, turning his twelve foot ceilings into nine—was unfinished, unkempt, and downright filthy.

Just the way he liked it.

Michael had to duck under the beams that made up the ceiling, and he used his hand to swipe away the myriad of cobwebs that blocked his path. The worn wooden steps groaned under his weight, and he stepped carefully, making sure not to scuff his loafers. Only six short steps later and he found himself on the concrete floor.

The lower level was more like a dungeon than the basement of a luxurious condo. This was his place, while the upstairs was just the shell's place—MGY's place, a place that he kept solely in order to keep up appearances.

He crouched on his haunches as he moved deeper into the darkness; at six foot two and with ceilings just a hair over five feet, Michael couldn't even come close to standing.

"Please...anything," the woman whispered again, this time her voice crystal clear. Michael followed her voice and made his way toward the east corner of the basement. As soon as he crossed the invisible sensor, a red light overhead clicked on, chasing the darkness with its pervasive glow. Out of habit, his eyes flicked up to the camera that was affixed to the corner of the room.

The record light had automatically turned on.

"Please..."

Only after he was satisfied that everything was working as intended did Michael turn his attention to the three-by-three-foot iron cube before him. It too had cost a pretty penny to make, and had cost him even more for the welder that had built it to keep quiet.

Inside, however, was the real prize. Inside, a blonde-haired woman in her mid-thirties sat huddled, her knees pressed tightly to her narrow chest. Her hair was damp and hung over her face, the visible parts of which were glistening from tears and sweat.

"I'll do anything," she whispered, raising her eyes to look at him. She was pretty, a businesswoman whom he had picked up two nights ago at a dive bar, probably out trying to get over a recent breakup. Her beige skirt and matching jacket, then immaculate and probably designer, had seemed so out of place in the grungy atmosphere filled with the odor of sour beer.

And that was it; all he'd had to do was spot that skirt and Michael had known that she would be an easy target.

But now, the dress, like the rest of her, was a soiled mess.

"Please," she pleaded desperately. Michael felt a pang of hunger in his stomach, despite the sparkling water he had consumed upstairs only a few short moments prior.

He didn't say anything; he rarely spoke to his victims. Instead, he observed. For a long while, Michael was content in simply holding her gaze.

Slowly, when it was clear that just staring at him was not going to affect the way she perhaps hoped it would, the woman tried another tactic.

She pulled her hands from her shins and held them out to him, palms up.

Michael's hunger pangs increased in intensity.

The skin from all ten of her fingers had been chewed off, revealing a horrible mess of coagulated blood speckled with patches of gleaming bone and grisly sinew.

Michael smiled, before reaching up and manually switching off the red light. It was only then that he noticed the plastic vent cover had come loose and was hanging.

And that explains why I could hear her upstairs.

He made a mental note to repair it more formally later, but for now he reached up and pushed it back into place. Finally, he returned his attention to the sobbing woman in the cage.

"Sorry, sweetie, not hungry enough yet. Soon, I promise."

The woman didn't scream, but as he made his way in his awkward half-squat half-standing walk back to the stairs, he heard her begin to sob again.

No, Michael Grant Young was not like everyone else. And he was dead set on letting the world know it. *Eventually.*

Just not today. Today he had other work to do.

Chapter 5

"FUCK!" CAL SCREAMED AS the man's thin, cold hands wrapped around his throat. He bucked his hips, and thankfully it appeared as if the quiddity had expended most of his horrible ghost energy sprinting like a madman.

The man literally flew off of him, grunting as he landed in a heap. Cal immediately scrambled to his feet, and began patting his chest, arms, legs, everything on his body to make sure it was all still there. As the quiddity groaned on the grass, Cal looked around desperately for his friends, who were rushing toward him.

"What the fuck happened, Allan?! What happened?!" he nearly shrieked. When the old man started to get to his feet, Cal aimed a finger at his chest. "Stay there! Stay down!" Then, to Allan, he added, "What a fucking stupid plan!"

The boy's face fell, but he kept walking toward him nonetheless.

Shelly got to him first.

"What happened, Cal? Did he—did he—?"

"Yes, he fucking touched me—what the hell!"

Shelly made a face, and she took a small step backward.

Cal didn't blame her.

"He didn't show up," Allan whispered. They were standing side by side now, staring down at the man who had finally managed to get to one knee.

"What?"

"The guy—this guy—he didn't show up."

"What the fuck are you talking about, Allan? What do you mean he didn't show up?"

Shelly grabbed Cal's arm, and the touch of another person made him jump.

"He means that the man isn't dead."

Cal blinked hard.

Not dead? This old man in the navy regalia wandering through the cemetery at midnight isn't dead?

"You," he said. The old man groaned and then collapsed into a seated position. "Hey, you!" Cal repeated.

"Me?" he said, looking up at him with a heavily-lined face.

"Yeah, you—you alive?"

The man looked confused, but then his expression hardened. "Where is my wife?" he demanded.

Allan reached down and picked up the camera on the tripod that had fallen when the man had attacked Cal.

"Give me the fucking camera," Cal ordered, snatching it from Allan's grasp. It was awkward to hold with the now bent tripod still attached, but when he brought the lens to his eye, it still seemed to work.

Allan was right; the man wasn't glowing. Cal could make out the grass and the tree, even the tombstone off to the old man's left. But the man himself was just a dark silhouette.

He pulled the camera away from his face for a quick inspection, before bringing it back to his eyes.

The result was the same.

"You sure it's not broken? Does this little trick of yours always work?"

"Always," Allan said.

"Then you are alive," Cal said quietly, as if trying to convince himself.

"Of course I'm alive, you jackass," the man said, trying and this time succeeding in standing. "Now tell me where my wife is."

Shelly stepped forward, hand outstretched.

"Listen, bud, we don't know who you are or what you're doing here, and we certainly haven't seen your wife, but you can't be here right now."

The man's response was immediate.

"The fuck I can't."

Then he turned his head skyward.

"Lorraine! Lorraine! Where are you, Lorraine?"

"Keep it down!" Shelly insisted. While it was unlikely that the shitty cemetery that they had chosen at the outskirts of Hainsey County had any security—in fact, this was the primary reason why they had chosen it—it was probably still best not to draw attention to themselves.

Nothing good could come out of being caught with all sorts of camera equipment in a cemetery at midnight. And given Cal's past and his problems with the law, well, that wouldn't help either.

The man ignored Shelly's pleas, and instead raised his voice as if to spite her.

"Lorraine! Lorraine Smith! Are you out here?"

"Shut the—"

But Cal stopped speaking when Allan grabbed his arm. He turned to face the man, and was surprised to see that his eyes were bulging from behind his circular spectacles.

"What?" Cal asked, shaking free of the man's grip. "What's wrong with you?"

"Lorraine," he whispered.

"So what?"

Allan extended a finger and pointed to a tombstone just outside the clearing where their three cameras were aimed.

"Lorraine," he repeated.

And then Cal realized what he meant.

"No shit," he whispered.

"No shit," Allan confirmed. Shelly, still unsure of what was going on, quickly moved to the tombstone that Allan was indicating, all the while keeping her eyes locked on the strange man in the navy regalia.

Cal watched her out of the corner of his eye. She swept away some of the dead leaves that hung from the tombstone, then whipped out her cell phone to use the flashlight. After moving her fingers over the engravings to clean out the dirt, she suddenly froze.

And Cal knew.

He didn't need Shelly to verbally confirm his suspicions, the expression on her face was sufficient.

The tombstone was of one Lorraine Smith.

"Um, mister?"

"Lorraine," the man shouted again. "Lorraine, where are you? I heard your voice!"

"Mister!"

Finally, the man's wrinkled face turned to Shelly.

"What? Do you know where she is?"

"Yeah," Shelly said quietly. "I know where she is. And I think we need to talk."

Chapter 6

"HEY THERE, SUNSHINE," CARSON said, leering at the man in the business suit. He was standing on the steps outside a massive glass skyscraper, the oversized aviator shades only just sufficient to block out the bright midday sun.

The man in the suit looked down at him, as he likely did with most everyone he met, and his handsome face twisted into a frown.

"Quit begging; I'm not giving you anything."

Carson could feel Jonah creeping up behind him, his breathing coming more rapidly, but he used his hand to keep the man at bay.

"Come on," he said, the smile still on his face. "Let's take a walk, Michael."

The man's eyes narrowed and his expression changed, transitioning from firm and disgusted to something akin to nervousness. There were several other people in suits milling about like little well-dressed ants following some pheromones or other secretions by an unseen queen, but while they all looked like Michael, they weren't like him.

Not in the least.

Michael had different...interests.

"Who are you?" Michael whispered.

"Just a guy who knows a guy." Carson waved an arm. "Come on, let's walk."

The man appeared hesitant, but whereas a few moments ago he'd been looking to his fellow suits for support, he was now looking to see if they were staring at him, as if they might overhear.

Carson's smile grew.

Different interests indeed.

Still, despite his pride at picking the guy out of the crowd, time was of the essence. Every day that Robert was out there was another day that Leland was trapped in the Marrow.

"Michael? Take a walk—I'm pretty sure it would be best if this video didn't come out with all of your peers milling about, don't you?" he asked calmly. The man's clean-shaven face suddenly dropped at the word videotape.

"Video? You—" Michael stammered.

Carson teased one of his hands out of the pocket of his spring coat just far enough to reveal the corner of a digital camera.

"Come on, now, Michael. Let's go for a walk."

The man in the suit took a hesitant step forward, his eyes wide.

***

"What is this? Extortion? If I don't do what you say, you're going to go to the police? Is that it?" Michael asked. The slick, perfect image that he had projected on the stairs of the eighty-story building had shattered. Sweat covered his face and brow, and his hair, perfectly groomed minutes before, was now a mess. He had pulled his tie loose and the top button of his shirt was undone.

Carson stared at him for a good ten seconds before answering.

"Do we look like the type of people who would go to the police?" he asked at last.

Jonah, who was sitting on the other side of Carson on the bench, snickered.

"What do you want, then? Money?"

Carson mulled this over for a moment. A normal person would have seen the video of Michael Young pushing the woman into the cage before starting to cut her, and then glance at the man in the suit beside him on the bench, and have said, 'Nuh-uh, no way, not the same person.'

But Carson looked into the man's eyes and he knew.

Neither of them were normal men.

"Join us."

Michael made a face.

"Join you? What are you talking about? Who the fuck are you guys?"

Carson shook his head.

"There is so much that you don't know, Mike. So much. And I can help you learn."

Michael stood, glancing around nervously. They had been sitting on a bench in a small park located just out of view from the large office buildings that comprised the financial district.

But the ants were in their hive, doing what they did; the park itself was empty.

"I don't know where the fuck you got that video from," Michael said, pointing at the outline of the camera that Carson had tucked back into his pocket. "And I don't know who the fuck you two clowns are, or what you wanted to accomplish coming here today, but it ain't happening."

Carson raised an eyebrow.

"It's not?"

Michael shook his head.

"No, no way. Look at you two guys." He waved a hand at Carson. "You look like a malnourished convict, and you" —he moved to Jonah next— "fuck, I don't even know what you look like."

Carson shrugged.

"Pretty close, actually." His eyes narrowed. "But before you go and say or do something that you will regret, let me ask you one question."

Michael opened his mouth to continue his diatribe, but then thought better of it and softened his tone.

"I'll buy the tape off you. You guys look like you need money. I have money."

Again, Carson shrugged.

"You're right, we need money. But, like I said, we need you more than we need your cash. Let me just ask you one question, can you give me that much, at least? Just one question?"

Michael hesitated, but eventually acquiesced.

"Shoot."

"Good. Well, Michael, when you kill these women, what do you see?"

Michael grimaced. Clearly, despite the video evidence, he was still unwilling to openly admit to what he had done.

What he still did.

"See? What do you mean, see?"

Michael took a small step backward.

"Don't play coy, Michael. What do you see in their eyes when they go? Huh? What is it that you see?"

Something changed in the man's face; it hardened, and the mask that he put on every morning suddenly became transparent, offering both Carson and Jonah a glimpse of the horrible demon beneath.

"Listen, you fucks. I'm going to leave this park now, and if I ever see either of you —"

Carson bolted to his feet, and Michael stumbled backward.

"I'm warning you..."

Jonah also stood. For such a stumpy man, he moved with unexpected dexterity. He silently slid a few steps to Michael's left. The latter had become so enraged that he didn't appear to notice.

Carson stepped toward the man sweating in his suit.

"I'll tell you what you see, Michael...I'll tell you what you see, and then you're going to join us. I'm going to open your mind to things that are greater than you ever thought possible."

Chapter 7

"WHAT'S YOUR NAME?" CAL asked the man in the navy regalia, who had quickly gone from furious to terrified after seeing his wife's grave. Despite being attacked by him earlier, Cal actually felt sorry for the confused and sad old man before him.

"Walter," he said softly. "Walter Smith. You mean you haven't seen her at all? You haven't seen Lorraine?"

Cal shook his head and took a step forward. Walter responded by taking an equally large step backward.

"I—I heard her, I swear I did."

Shelly, who was now standing beside Cal, spoke next, her tone soft, soothing. Clearly, she felt compassion for Walter as well.

"Walter, your wife…your wife passed some time ago."

The man's eyes shot up, but it wasn't surprise that Cal saw in them, but frustration.

"I know," he said curtly. "She died a year ago to the day. But I heard her. I was on my way to visit her grave—dressed in the same navy uniform that we were married in—when I heard her voice call to me."

Cal checked his watch.

"You were coming here? Now? At midnight?"

Shelly elbowed him in the ribs, and he grunted. Walter Smith, however, was unfazed by the comment.

"Lorraine died almost exactly at midnight—in her sleep, God rest her soul."

"Yeah, that God rest her soul bit? That's something we need to talk about."

Again, Shelly elbowed him in the ribs, this time hard enough for him to cry out. He turned to her.

"What?" he demanded angrily.

Shelly didn't answer, but instead stepped between Cal and Walter.

"Was your wife buried over there?" she asked, hooking a finger at the plain ash-gray tombstone that bore the woman's name.

Walter looked confused.

"Yes, that's her tombstone. Why?"

"I mean, was she buried? As in, did you see her lowered into the ground?"

The man finally seemed to catch on to what she was asking. He shook his head slowly.

"No, Lorraine was cremated—even brought her ashes with me. Was going to sprinkle a little bit on her grave every year until I pass. That way I never forget, you know?"

Shelly nodded.

"You brought the urn with you?"

Cal furrowed his brow.

What's she getting at?

Walter nodded, and then looked back to the area from which he had rushed at Cal.

"Over there. But what does this have to do with Lorraine—with me hearing Lorraine's voice?" He lowered his head. "Am I going mad?"

Shelly immediately took another step forward, and then indicated for Allan to head over to where Walter had said he had set down the urn and retrieve it.

"No, Walter, I don't think you are going mad. I think that you really did hear your late wife."

"But...how is that possible?"

Shelly moved right up next to Walter now, and gently laid her hand on his shoulder. Walter immediately slumped; his navy gear, which had been worn with such pride when he had first entered the cemetery, now hung off of his wiry frame like ill-fitting pajamas. It was as if he had used up all his energy coming here and then charging at Cal, and now that he was spent, his body had simply withered.

"It's possible," Shelly said just loud enough for Cal to hear. She looked over her shoulder at him, and he saw something in her eyes that he didn't care for. Cal took a step forward, trying to intervene before she made a horrible mistake, but as usual, he was late to the party. "And you can see her again, Walter. You can see your wife one last time."

***

"This is fucking insane, Shel. Like, seriously stupid. Worse than even Allan's idea of coming out here in the first place."

Shelly bit her lip.

"We have to try."

"No, no we don't. We don't have to try anything. We could just leave all of this stuff behind us, live off the money that Sean gave us and do something else."

It was Allan who piped up next.

"I can't do that."

Cal turned to him, trying hard to keep his voice low so that the man in the clearing couldn't hear what he was saying.

"You can't? You? I distinctly remember you whimpering like a little boy who lost his pacifier back at Seaforth—back when Sean brought us there and locked us in the closet. Do you remember that?"

Allan lowered his gaze.

"And this—" He gestured to the camera setup and Walter, who was now sitting in the center of the clearing. "—this seems a lot like that, doesn't it? Like how Sean used us as bait to get

Robert to come to Seaforth. You know that, right? This seems almost exactly like that."

Shelly suddenly tossed the urn at him, and Cal swore as he juggled the slick black vase. After nearly dropping it, he somehow managed to grab it with both hands.

"Shelly! What the fuck!" he huffed, sweat breaking out on his brow. "What's wrong with you?"

Shelly ignored the question and just stared at him for a moment. Cal stared back. She was dressed in ultra-tight leather pants, and was sporting a black spring jacket over top a very low-cut black V-neck, revealing the tops of her breasts. It was an outfit he had seen her wear before—Shelly had a minimalist wardrobe, if there ever was one—but it seemed different now; the pants seemed tighter in the thighs, and he had some serious doubts that she would have been able to do up the jacket had it been a cooler night. In fact, all of her clothes seemed to be tighter, and he wondered, not for the first time, if he should actively encourage her to join him in his workouts; it seemed that every pound he lost, she gained some of it.

It was her drinking; her drinking had kicked into high gear ever since Robert had abandoned them.

"What?" he said at last, unable to hold her gaze for any longer.

"You feel that?"

Cal gripped the urn tightly in both hands.

"Yes, of course I feel it. It feels like—"

Shelly reached out and snatched it from him before he could react. Extra weight or not, she could still be quick when she needed to.

"When my parents died, they were cremated. I held both of their urns." Her voice hitched almost imperceptibly, and Cal's expression softened.

He had had no idea that Shelly's parents were dead. In fact, other than the stuff that he had read online—about her living in Montreal prior to joining them in the Harlop Estate, and being a source of knowledge when it came to the quiddity—he realized in that moment that he knew very little about Shelly.

In fact, he knew little about Shelly, about Sean, or about Allan. He looked at the young man next, but couldn't get a read on him; Allan was staring at Walter, who at some point during their argument had wrapped his arms over his knees like a child.

The only person Cal knew was Robert, but given the way things had gone…well, he wasn't so sure about that anymore, either.

"Anyway," Shelly continued, her voice hardening. "The urn is too light."

"What do you mean, too light?"

She lowered her voice and moved even closer.

"It's too light—meaning, not all of her is in there."

Cal finally caught her drift.

"What a minute, you think—you think—" He shook his head. "No, no way."

Shelly turned to Allan.

"Allan, what do you think?"

"It's possible," he admitted with a shrug. "I mean, if they didn't cremate all of her body, then maybe her quiddity can still be trapped here. Can't say for certain, but it's possible." Allan didn't take his eyes off Walter as he spoke. "He said he heard her, and given what we've seen…"

"Jesus fucking Christ," Cal swore. "So, what, we just sit here and wait for the poor bastard's dead wife to visit? Then we try your crazy camera trick to trap her?"

"Robert's not coming back, Cal; we can't rely on him with his fucking superpowers, or whatever he did at Seaforth, to keep the quiddity at bay. We need to try this—to try something. Just in case."

Cal had to fight the urge to pull out his hair.

"Just in case? Jesus, are you listening to yourself right now?" Despite his admonition, Cal was acutely aware of the irony of his words.

Before Walter had rushed at him and he was certain that he was going to be transported to the Marrow, Cal had used the same twisted logic to convince himself to come to the cemetery in the first place.

But now that he heard the idea verbalized, it sounded absurd.

Shelly pressed her lips together tightly. Clearly, she felt differently.

"It's not up to you, anyway—Allan and I are doing this. Feel free to leave at any time."

With that, she spun on her heels, and started walking toward Walter, holding the urn out in front of her.

For a moment, Cal just stared, incredulous.

Then he snapped out of it.

"Wait!" he said finally. "Shelly, just wait!"

Chapter 8

MICHAEL TOOK MUCH MORE persuading than Jonah, which had set them back longer than Carson had hoped or even expected. It was partly because he had never met the man before—unlike Jonah, with whom he had crossed paths several times before being incarcerated—and partly because the man was naturally suspicious. A good thing, Carson supposed, given their business. Jonah, on the other hand…

Carson had persisted because Michael was important—important because he had something that neither he nor Jonah had: money, and lots of it. And no matter how much Carson loathed the pursuit of the all-mighty dollar, he was a practical man.

Money would come in handy; money could be used to buy people off, money could be used to buy weapons, money could be used to buy a fucking drink.

So despite the setback, Carson couldn't help but allow the smile that tickled the inside of his cheeks to grow. And sitting in the front seat of Michael's luxury Mercedes, why shouldn't he smile?

"Where we off to next, Carson?" Jonah asked from the backseat. "When are we going to get some action?"

Carson didn't answer at first. He was suddenly put off by the little man, mostly because his excited demeanor reminded him of Buddy. And that type of attitude had made Buddy sloppy, and it was what got him arrested.

And then executed.

Carson thought back to his and Buddy's first kill together, how they had set up a tent just outside the city in Green Mountain National Forest. They had chosen September, because temperatures were dropping and yet it wasn't cold enough to deter all visitors. Still, it took longer than he had expected to identify their victim, which was perhaps why he had so much patience today.

The same couldn't be said about Buddy.

Hunkered in the thin forest just off a worn hiking path, it was nearly two hours before the first person—a man with his dog—finally walked by.

Of course, Buddy wanted to pounce, to just leap out of the trees and grab the man. But Carson wanted to wait. And when the man's dog took a big shit, and the dutiful parkgoer leaned down to pick it up with a bag, his jacket pulled up a bit, revealing a blue tattoo on his wrist.

"Now?" Buddy whispered.

Carson put his hand on his friend's shoulder, holding him back. The tattoo on the man's wrist had been Army insignia. Carson was young back then, young and stupid, but he knew enough not to mess with military men.

"No, not him," he told his friend. "Let him go."

Buddy's round face soured.

"Why not?"

Carson shook his head.

"He's military."

Buddy was incredulous. And bloodthirsty. Man, Buddy was the most bloodthirsty individual Carson had ever come across, even compared to him and his other inmates at Seaforth.

Bloodthirsty to the point of being careless. And look where that got him.

"Military? So? There are two of us—we can take him."

Back then, Buddy had been more muscle than fat—something that changed dramatically over the years—and at a hefty six feet, Carson didn't doubt his friend's words.

"I know, but not him."

"Why the fuck not?"

Buddy also had a temper, which was liable to bubble over at any moment. And that moment was close, Carson could just feel it.

"Because if we fuck with him, then we are fucking with all of his Army brat friends. You want that? You want to be hunted for the rest of our lives, always looking over our shoulders for men in fatigues? That sound like fun to you?"

A couple of discharged soldiers with PTSD were frequent visitors to his step-parents' crack den. Even these drug-addled men showed an almost supernatural persistence. If they took out an Army brat with their first kill together, there was no stopping his comrades' thirst for revenge.

It was a clichéd thing to say, but it seemed to work. Buddy's expression softened.

"Let's just wait for an easier target, shall we?"

Buddy agreed.

They didn't have to wait long for the second passerby. Less than ten minutes later, a woman in her mid-forties sporting a bright yellow vest and a black headband over her ears jogged by.

She was their first, and Carson would never forget her.

"Carson? Where to next? Can we get some now?"

Carson scowled at having been drawn out of his reverie.

"No, not yet. Keep your dick in your pants, Jonah. There will be more action than you know what to deal with."

"But I want it now," Jonah whined. He was like a child wrapped up in a fat man's body.

"Jonah, shut the fuck up."

Michael spoke up next.

"You need to tell me where I'm driving to, and you need to also tell me what the hell your master plan is."

Carson almost chuckled out loud. These two couldn't possibly comprehend his 'master plan.' They were but pawns, and a king never told his disciples all of his secrets. Still, it was clear that with Michael the same promises of spilling blood that he had made to Jonah were insufficient. The man was a killer, the video proved as much, but he was a cautious killer. A calculated one, one that avoided risks. And, as a consequence, one that avoided prison as well.

"There is one more person we need to get, then we can sit down and have a chat."

"One more?" Jonah asked from the backseat, his voice increasing in pitch.

"One more," Carson confirmed. "A woman."

Carson caught a glimpse of the sneer that crossed Jonah's face in the rearview mirror.

No, not that kind, Jonah. This isn't the type of girl you want to try something with.

***

Carson found Bella exactly where he'd known she would be: at their favorite bar, sipping her favorite drink. A Bloody Mary, go figure.

With Michael and Jonah waiting in the car, he entered the bar and approached her from behind. Even though he hadn't seen Bella in nearly a decade, he knew it was her despite only seeing the back of her head and her shoulders. And that was even considering that she was wearing a gray turtleneck sweater. He knew it was her not just because he recognized her straight, black hair that fell to just below her shoulders, or that rose tattoo in the webbing of her right hand that gripped the Bloody Mary, but he knew because of the way she sat. Even though she was on a barstool, her back was perfectly straight, her posture the envy of all but the most prestigious of finishing schools.

This was Bella alright, and God how he'd missed her.

Instead of giving himself away, Carson elected to silently slide in beside her instead.

As expected, she didn't even bother raising her head to look at him.

The barkeep, an older man with deep grooves around his nose and mouth and perfectly shellacked white hair, came over to him.

His voice was a perfect match for his appearance.

"What can I get ya?"

Carson smiled. It had been a really, really long time since he had seen Bella, and it had been even longer since he had had a drink. But while Bella was always partial to her Bloody Marys, he was more of a bourbon guy.

"A double of Bulleit. Neat," he replied simply.

The ring on Bella's second finger, a simple, silver band that Carson had given her long ago, suddenly stopped tapping against the side of her glass.

Then, almost in slow motion, Bella turned to face him.

"Oh, hi, Bella, fancy finding you here," he said with a grin.

Bella's dark brown eyes bulged and the glass slipped from her hand.

"Carson? Carson?"

Chapter 9

WHEN SHELLY GOT THIS way, there was nothing anyone—not Cal, not Allan, and not even Robert—could say to change her mind. So Cal reluctantly agreed to help her with the "plan."

Despite what he had said about wanting to leave this world, to run from this dangerous game that they were playing, deep down, he was relieved that they had decided to remain ensconced in it, at least for the time being. He didn't kid himself; after what he had seen at Seaforth and the Seventh Ward, he knew that there was a chance—a big chance—that he was risking death, or worse. But all of this was like a drug to him. The adrenaline he felt, and to a lesser degree the vindication for the scorn that had been thrown at him for even mentioning some of his 'conspiracy theories,' was something that he longed for.

There was also his best friend dying in his arms—there was always that. Robert might have been the one to go to the Marrow, might have walked on the shores and returned to talk about it when nobody else had, but Cal had seen it. He had fucking seen it, and he wanted to see it again. Only he wanted to do so on his own terms. And he wanted to come back—yeah, he really wanted to return to this world.

He leaned in close and whispered in Walter's ear.

"No matter what, you can't touch her. Remember that, Walter. No matter what."

The man looked up at him with sad, yet surprisingly clear eyes. Cal hadn't asked his age, but he pegged the man in his early eighties. For as old as he was, he seemed of particularly sound mind, which helped ease some of the guilt that built inside him.

"No matter what," Cal repeated, before gently placing a hand on his shoulder and stepping back.

"C'mon, Cal, we need to get started."

Cal held the man's gaze a little longer, making sure that the importance of his words sunk in. It was Walter who eventually broke the stare, pretending to have to adjust the urn between his hands.

As per the plan, if you could call it such, Cal retreated to his camera. And then, once behind the lens, they were like they had been before Walter had arrived: Cal, Shelly, and Allan behind their cameras, all focused on the area upon which they triangulated. Only this time, there was a man sitting in the center. A sad, sad man who only wanted to desperately see his wife again.

Cal shook his head, trying to remain focused.

"Okay," Shelly said, her voice soft. "Call out to her. Tell her you are by her grave."

Walter closed his eyes for a moment, and when he opened them again, something had changed in him, something was different.

Cal felt a sudden impending sense of dread.

"Lorraine?" Walter said softly. "Lorraine, I'm here. I'm here by your grave. I came because you called."

Almost instantly, there was a rustling off to the man's left, just behind a large oak tree. Shelly had set up several portable lights by the clearing, but had turned all but one of them off to avoid spooking Lorraine. But now Cal wished that she had kept them all on. He squinted hard, but there was barely any moonlight illuminating the tree, and even less the shadows behind.

His heart started to race.

Fuck, fuck, fuck.

He felt the familiar tingle in his fingertips, and sweat began to form on his forehead despite the cool temperature outside.

"Lorraine?" Walter asked, the pitch of his voice increasing ever so slightly. "Is that you?"

A raccoon suddenly darted out of the shadows, and Cal felt all of the air in his lungs whoosh out. He hadn't meant to exhale loudly, but he had, and it spooked the nocturnal creature, which quickly scampered into the darkness.

"Walt?" The voice was thin, wavery, bordering on tinny.

Cal whipped his head around to the other side of their setup, this time the air getting stuck in his throat.

There was a woman in a white, nearly iridescent nightgown, walking toward Walter and the urn. As Cal watched, she moved farther into the clearing, her feet seeming to slide across the grass as opposed to stepping through it. Her eyes were fixed on Walter, and as Shelly had predicted, the woman with long black hair that ran nearly midway down her back didn't even notice them.

In fact, she didn't appear to notice the light that Shelly had set up, either.

Wait for the signal, he chided himself.

His finger was twitching uncontrollably, mere millimeters above the shutter-release button.

Walter was facing the wrong way, but at the sound of his wife's voice, he swiveled to face her. When their eyes met, he dropped the urn on the grass.

"Lorraine!" Walter rubbed his eyes like a kid on Christmas morning. "Lorraine, is that really you?"

The woman's pace increased and her face, even more heavily lined than the old man's, brightened.

"Oh, Walter, it is you! I've been — I've been so confused ever since you left me."

Left me?

Cal felt his heart beating wildly in his chest as Walter pushed himself to his feet.

They were only five or six feet apart now.

Cal let his finger brush up against the trigger, but didn't press it, not just yet.

'Wait until she is at least within two feet of Walter—no earlier,' Allan had instructed.

With bated breath, Cal waited, so rapt in the scene unfolding before him that he didn't even consider looking over at Shelly or Allan.

"I've missed you, Walt. Really missed you. Every night I come here, wander in these woods, among the tombstones, looking for you. I'm so sorry about what happened."

Lorraine took another sliding step forward, then another.

Four feet now, maybe less.

Cal had never fired a gun before, but he had heard of an itchy trigger finger. That was exactly what he had now: an itchy trigger finger.

He just wanted to snap the picture and then tell Walter to get the hell out of there.

"Where...where have you been? Why did you leave me, Walter?"

It dawned on Cal that Walter hadn't spoken for several minutes, and he suddenly feared for the man's heart. His face was pale, seemingly drained of all blood, and his eyes were wide. Even Cal, despite everything that he had seen, everything he knew about this world, he still had a hard time digesting the fact that this woman was dead—his mind rejected the idea, reverting to the tenets that he had been indoctrinated with at an early age. You live, you die, you go to Heaven or Hell. There was no coming back. And if he felt this way, he couldn't even imagine what poor Walter was thinking or feeling.

"I hear this voice, a voice calling to me...a man's voice, telling me that I need to come to the Sea, that he can help me learn the truth. He calls himself...he calls himself the Goat, Walter. And I'm scared."

Cal felt his blood run cold.

The Goat. Robert's father.

"What does it all mean, Walt? Why don't—?"

When she took another step toward the silent man, Cal could hold his finger no longer.

He clicked the trigger button, and he heard the camera shutter close.

At first, nothing happened. The viewfinder still showed a bright red-and-orange outline of Lorraine's form, which in and of itself was unsettling. The actual man, the living, breathing man, showed up as a blurry outline, but this quiddity, Lorraine's confused, disoriented soul that was solicited by Leland Black, was as vibrant as a supernova.

"Now!" Allan shouted, and Cal, who had jumped the gun, just kept on mashing the button.

"Walt? Whaaaaaaaaaat issssssssss happppennninng?"

Her voice slowed, the individual words drawn out. It wasn't as deliberate as what had happened at Seaforth when Robert had demanded the quiddity to stop, but something was clearly happening. It was as if Lorraine was suddenly moving through ether.

"Shel? Allan?" Cal shouted, still unwilling to take his eyes off Lorraine and Walter. "What's going on?"

There was no immediate answer.

As he watched, Lorraine suddenly stopped moving entirely. It appeared as if her entire being had frozen solid, her eyes still open, her lips pressed together as if in mid-word.

"Shel?"

"Move away from her, Walter," Shelly piped up. Cal, drawn by the sound of her voice, was alarmed to see that she had stepped away from her camera and was moving toward the clearing.

"Shelly? What's happening? Stay behind the camera, Shelly."

"Lorraine...how I've loathed you," Walter suddenly snarled. "After what you did, I came back here to kill you again."

Cal whipped his head back toward the scene, and was shocked to see an expression of sheer fury on Walter's face.

"What the fu—?"

"No!" Shelly suddenly screamed, and then she started sprinting toward Lorraine and Walter. Cal, still confused, was helpless to prevent himself from doing the same.

"I found the letters, you slut. It wasn't just one time, was it? I can't believe that you—"

Then Walter did the unfathomable. Despite countless warnings, Walter reached out and grabbed his dead, frozen wife by the throat.

"No!" Cal shouted. But he was too late.

With his long, thin fingers grasping the wrinkled skin of her throat, Walter's head suddenly snapped back and his mouth opened in a long, horrible wail.

Then he started to shake and his eyes started to go black.

Chapter 10

"PAROLE," CARSON SAID WITH a laugh.

Bella gaped.

"No."

Carson's continued to laugh.

"No, of course not."

Bella took a sip from the new drink that the barkeep had made for her, all the while staring at him. Her reaction wasn't exactly the adulation that he had expected.

"Bella," he said, leaning in close to her. When she pulled back, he had to use all of his willpower to resist the frown that threatened to surface. "It's me Bella. It's really me."

But despite his claims, Bella seemed unconvinced. When he reached out to touch her hand, she pulled back so quickly that she nearly toppled off the barstool. And then he understood; the fear in her face said it all.

"Ha, okay, I get it now. I'm not dead, Bella. I am not one of them."

Bella squinted at him.

"How can I know? I mean, before you were put away…you remember the dreams, don't you? The ones you told me about? About the" —she lowered her voice—"the sea?"

Carson rubbed his chin.

"Bella, I know so much more now, so much more about this entire existence than you can ever imagine…I've seen—I've seen it, Bella, I've seen the shores of the Marrow. And I've seen him, Bella. There is so much more that you don't know."

He could see the sparkle return to her eyes, but she still wasn't smiling. Her guard was still up.

"Fine," Carson said with a wink, "I know how to prove to you that I'm real. Barkeep?"

The man gave a curt nod and came over. His thin lips were twisted into a sour expression, which was odd given the fact that Carson and Bella were his only patrons.

"What can I do you for?" he said, eying their nearly full drinks.

"Tequila. Best you got."

When the bartender didn't move right away, Carson remembered what Michael had called him when they first met.

'You look like an anorexic convict.'

Carson reached into his wallet and pulled out the wad of cash that he had persuaded Michael to take out of the ATM. He tossed a fifty onto the bar.

Unsurprisingly, the bartender's expression suddenly changed, his eyes going wide at the sight of the cash. He quickly reached down, pulled a bottle of Tequila Bang Bang from somewhere out of sight, and put it beside two shot glasses on the bar.

"Seriously?" Bella asked, her thin eyebrows lifting.

"You don't want it?" the barkeep asked, the grimace threatening to return.

"No, it's fine. It'll bring us back, what do you say, Bella? A shot for old times' sake?"

Bella shrugged. She was pretty, in a non-traditional sense. It was her hair, Carson realized, that made her bump the line from average to pretty, what with it being so shiny and straight. When he had first met her all those years ago during her internship in the juvie facility that Carson was held at, he had longed to touch that hair, to feel if it was as silky as it looked.

It was.

Since that day, he had touched a lot more than just her hair.

Staring at Bella, Carson felt an unfamiliar tightness to the front of his pants. It had been a long, long time since he had been with a woman.

The barkeep poured the shots, but just as he was finishing the second one, Carson, eyes still locked on Bella, reached out and grabbed the man's hand that was holding the neck of the tequila bottle.

"Hey!" the barkeep cried, and immediately tried to jerk his hand away. Carson's grip held fast. He turned his attention to the bartender, who was oblivious to the fact that the shot glass was overflowing, spilling sour-smelling tequila all over the bar.

The man's wide eyes were locked on Carson's sneer.

"Next time I ask you for a drink, you best get it right away. Got it? That, you can do me for."

The bartender again tried to pull his hand away, but Carson's fingers dug deep into his wrist.

"Got it?" he repeated between clenched teeth.

"G-g-got it," the man stammered.

Only then did Carson release his hand, which sent the barkeep stumbling backward. Carson ignored him as he righted the bottle, then set about cleaning up the spilled tequila without another word.

"See? I'm very much alive, Bella. And there is so much I need to tell you. So drink up, because it's gonna be a long night."

***

"This will do nicely," Carson said as he looked around the dingy basement of Scarsdale Crematorium. The walls were covered in grime and years of ashes from burnt bodies, and the lights were so dim that they barely cut splinters through the gloom. It looked different from the last time he had been here, when the fire had been raging. It would never be featured in Home and Garden, but that suited him just fine. "And you're sure that the other guy that works here—Vinny—won't give us any problems?"

Jonah scratched at his stomach and grunted.

"No, no problems from him, that's for sure."

"And they'll just keep bringing bodies?"

"Yep. They bring 'em, I burn 'em."

Michael scoffed. Clearly, he was less impressed by Scarsdale than Carson.

"Look, Carson, are you going to tell me what we're doing here? Let me in on what the fucking plan is? Because I get the feeling that I don't quite fit in here, if you know what I mean?" Michael looked down at his bespoke navy suit, then glanced over at Jonah, who was wearing a Mickey Mouse t-shirt that was speckled with moth holes and was a couple sizes too small.

Carson smiled.

How wrong you are, Michael. How very wrong—you are definitely right where you belong.

Carson leaned over and wrapped his arm around Bella's waist. He pulled her in tight and kissed her on the forehead.

Alone time—we're going to need some alone time soon.

"Look, Michael, you belong here. We—" He made a grandiose gesture to include all four of them. "—we are all the same."

He looked down at Bella when he spoke again.

"It's a new time, ladies and gentlemen. It's the dawn of a new era—and we are responsible for opening the floodgates. Soon everyone like us, every single person who is sick of conforming to societal norms, of hiding in their skin, of burying their self, will be free—both living and dead."

Carson smiled broadly as he finished his unplanned soliloquy. The response wasn't quite what he'd expected: Michael just stared at him, unblinking as a fish.

"What the fuck are you talking about?" the man exclaimed at last. "What in God's name are you saying?"

Michael's perfectly manicured brow suddenly furrowed and he took a step toward Carson. Jonah immediately moved to intervene. This time, unlike at the park by his office, Michael took notice.

"Look, I agreed to come here, to pick up your girlfriend, to give you some cash, but unless you let me in on your little secret, then this is where I draw the line. Tape or no tape."

Carson looked from Jonah to Bella, and then finally his eyes returned to Michael.

It wouldn't hurt if they knew the truth, he supposed. *After all, they will find out eventually—everyone finds out in the end.*

But it didn't have to be that way. If they got their shit together, they could change things…if they could only draw his brother out again, they could use him to open the gate.

An image of Robert suddenly flashed in his mind, the man's hand trembling as he aimed the gun at Carson's head. But Robert hadn't found it in himself to pull the trigger, to kill his brother.

Carson, however, wouldn't have the same issue if the tables were turned.

It had been clear, in that moment, with the hole in Father Callahan's head still smoldering, that Robert thought he was different than Carson. Better, maybe. But the fact was that it was Robert who had shot and killed Father Callahan, not Carson. Sure, in doing so he had closed the gate, and the priest was practically dead already, but Robert had murdered him.

And now that his brother had had a taste, Carson Ford very much doubted that he would be able to go much longer before he was compelled to do it again.

Once you felt the power, the euphoria of watching their quiddity pass out of their shell...

"Take a seat, Michael—we need to chat. Then we need to get started. Time is of the essence, my good folk. And it's a-wasting."

Chapter 11

"FUCK!" SHELLY SHOUTED AS she sprinted toward the clearing. Cal ran after her, but in the back of his mind, he had no idea what he was going to do once he got there.

"Shel! Wait!"

But Cal was spared a difficult decision; Walter and Lorraine faded before Shelly could make it to them, their bodies reduced to a thin mist reminiscent of the ashes that rested in the urn on the grass. And then that too disappeared, leaving Shelly alone in the clearing.

She turned back, and Cal saw a deep sadness in her eyes.

"Shit," she said softly. Her shoulders sagged, her head drooped.

Cal stared at her, barely recognizing that Allan had suddenly appeared at his side. Part of him felt like it was all Walter's fault—after all, he had been explicit about not touching his wife—but the nagging guilt wouldn't go away, not completely.

They had put him up to this crazy plan.

"We shouldn't have done this," Shelly whispered.

Cal bit his tongue, and thankfully Allan spoke up before he said something he would probably regret.

I fucking told you—and if I'm the voice of reason, Shelly, then we have real fucking problems.

"What have we done?" Allan asked, his voice airy.

Shelly's eyes shot up.

"We sent that man to the worst possible hell. And you heard what Sean said, every person that goes there, every person that stays on the shores, fuels Leland—gives him power." Her eyes went dark, her guilt transitioning seamlessly to anger. "You guys think that because of what happened at Seaforth that this is all over?" She waved her hands around, gesturing to the red urn first, then the cameras, then to them. "It doesn't matter that Carson is dead—Leland won't stop. As long as he is still in the Marrow, he won't ever stop."

She sighed. When she spoke again, it was as if there was a massive weight on her chest, pushing down on her, constricting her breathing.

"Not ever."

Cal swallowed hard. He knew her words to be true, despite the fact that he was still thoroughly confused as to what exactly had happened in Seaforth.

What he did know was that he and Allan had been lured to the prison by that bastard Sean; he had manipulated him—them—had used their own emotions against them, and then sequestered them in the small room, forbidding them to exit. Allan had been terrified, and it had taken much cajoling to convince the man to enter into the hallway. Three times they had ventured out, but his camera had revealed quiddity everywhere—more than he had ever seen, or so he claimed. Like cowards, they had remained holed up for hours, a day even, as the lights flicked on and off, as the screams echoed up and down the prison walls.

The sound that the makeshift ropes had made as they twisted and then snapped the necks of the guards still echoed in his mind. But that wasn't the worst part. The worst part was that he could still hear their desperate gasps in the adjacent mess hall while he and Allan sat cowering in silence.

"Cal? Why you crying, Cal?" Shelly asked. She made her way to him and pulled him into an embrace.

"We need Robert," he said simply. "Where the fuck did he go?"

Although Shelly didn't reply, he felt her nod in agreement.

Eventually Shelly pulled away, and Cal wiped the tears from his face and collected himself with a heavy breath.

They needed Robert, certainly, but even without him, they had work to do. Shelly was right, Leland wouldn't stop just because one of his sons had died.

After all, he had two.

Cal rubbed his eyes.

"That was fucked up," he said, and Shelly nodded in agreement. "But, Allan, did it work? I mean, something happened to Lorraine, didn't it?"

Allan nodded, and then adjusted his spectacles before speaking.

"Yeah, it worked—I think. I mean, she was frozen in place. It wasn't as fast as back at Seaforth, but…"

"That's what I saw, too," Shelly agreed. "But for how long? And, even more importantly, why did it work?"

Allan shook his head.

"Don't know for certain. I think that the lenses work kind of like thermal cameras, although the quiddity don't seem to give off much heat." He turned to Cal. "Remember in Seaforth? How cold it got when the cameras lit up?"

Cal nodded.

"So it must be something else. I mean, not everyone can even see them, right? So the cameras must somehow pick up a trace of whatever they are made of. And whatever they're made of, they leave a little bit behind, which is why I knew that the Harlop Estate had been haunted." He shrugged. "Maybe by having two or three cameras with the lenses focused on them and we take a picture, it locks whatever they are made of in place."

"Unless they go to the Marrow," Shelly said.

"Maybe. But even if that were true, it raises more questions than answers. I mean, how do they actually get to the Marrow?

The Goat is dead set on opening a rift, one big enough to allow him and his spirits to come back, but these rifts happen all the time—every time someone dies and they go to the Marrow, they have to travel via some sort of rift. But not all of them goes. They still leave a bit behind that I can track with my cameras. Here, let me show you."

Allan made his way over to his camera, and flipped the screen for them all to see.

"This is a live image," he said, "and Lorraine and Walter haven't been here for, what? Five? Ten minutes?"

Cal nodded. He wasn't sure where Allan was coming up with this shit, let alone why he hadn't told them before, and he wasn't sure how much of it was actually true, but it seemed plausible.

And based on what he had seen, plausible was enough.

"And yet"—Allan traced the faded red outline of a woman in the clearing with his finger—"here she is."

"Not as dark as at the Harlop Estate."

Allan shook his head.

"No, not as dark. But Lorraine was only here for a short time…and look, it's already fading."

"Like a fart in the wind," Cal said quietly.

Shelly turned to him, her lips pressed together tightly.

"Seriously? Joking at a time like this?"

Cal shrugged; it was his way of dealing with the pain and confusion coursing through him.

Allan ignored the both of them and continued.

"And there's something else, too. I took a video at Seaforth."

Cal felt the blood drain from his face. He remembered Allan's mangled mess of a camera in the helicopter, complete with a bullet hole in the casing. He hadn't even considered the possibility that any of what it had captured had been usable.

Allan must have seen the look on his face, as he nodded, his expression grim.

"Most was destroyed — mostly just the audio was saved. But I managed to salvage part of the video — a small clip, thirty seconds or so."

Cal swallowed hard.

"What part?" he whispered.

Allan paused, his eyes moving from Shelly to Cal, and then back again.

"The part where Robert orders the quiddity to stop — in the mess hall."

A silence fell over the trio as each of them struggled, and failed, to avoid recalling the horrors that they had witnessed at Seaforth Prison.

A shudder racked through Cal as he remembered the smell of the blood and gore that had been piled on top of him.

That was his second cowardly act of the day.

"And? What did it show?" he asked in a small voice.

Allan hesitated.

"You're not going to believe it — I need to show you. Let's pack up here and head back to the estate."

Chapter 12

DESPITE THE MAN'S DISTRUSTING nature and obvious apprehension, Carson knew that Michael was in. After all, for someone who had killed as many people as the financial banker by day had, he must have seen it in his victims' eyes. He must have seen their quiddity.

"We can open the rift, Michael, and then you can show people who you really are. It's a shame that you need to hide—that we are just supposed to succumb to societal constraints."

Michael's brow furrowed, his gaze shifting from Carson to Jonah and then Bella. When his hand suddenly snaked upward and went into the inside pocket of his suit jacket, Jonah immediately jumped to his feet. But instead of pulling out a weapon of some sort, he pulled his arm out of the jacket sleeve. Then he removed the other one.

The man meticulously and deliberately removed and placed the jacket gently, almost tenderly, on the back of his chair. It was an absurd charade, as the jacket had numerous stains peppering the navy fabric from the dingy Scarsdale Crematorium basement, and the chair itself, a primitive, wire-mesh design that was as ugly as it was uncomfortable, was just plain filthy.

Michael removed his tie next, and then he started unbuttoning his shirt.

"What are you doing?" Jonah demanded, but Carson hushed the little troll.

And when he saw what was beneath the man's shirt, Carson's smile grew until his cheeks started to hurt.

Michael's entire torso, from his belt to the hollow of his throat, from his navel to his wrists, was completely covered in tattoos. Dark blue ink spread outward from the center of chest forming intricate designs, faces, words, a complete and utter smorgasbord of ink that caused both Bella and Jonah to exhale sharply. Ignoring their reactions, Michael walked to the front of the chair and sat down.

"If it means I can show the world my real skin, then count me in," he said with a grin.

Carson clapped his hands together, the sound so loud in the basement that both Bella and Jonah jumped.

"Good to have you on board," he said, "I knew you'd come along for the ride."

"What now?" he asked, flexing his considerable chest. The man was in excellent shape, having obviously taken great care of the vessel that he so despised.

Carson stood.

"First off, we need some more help. Jonah, how many bodies do you have in the crematorium right now?"

Jonah thought about the question for a moment.

"There were four bodies to burn—not including Mrs. Kyra— when we left to get Michael and Bella," he said, "and we've been gone two days. I figure eight? Maybe nine, total?"

Bella took the initiative and strode over to the oven and peered around the side where the body bags were stacked.

"Well, your pal Vinny must have been busy; there are eleven bags here."

Even better.

"It's a start, it's a start," Carson said, more to himself than to the others. "I need some quiet now. I'm going to reach out to the other side—hopefully he will let me know how many we are going to need."

"He? What's the plan, Carson?" Michael asked. The man was insatiable.

"We need a Guardian to open the rift—only a Guardian stuck between two worlds can open it. And the Guardian we are going to use is my brother. Problem is" —his mind flicked back to Robert's face and his trembling hand clutching the gun—"he's not too keen on helping out. And, besides, I don't know where he is. After we find him, we will corner him with quiddity to keep him there."

Bella nodded in agreement.

"So first we find Robert, then all we need is to get some dead people to help us out?" Michael asked.

Carson ignored the sarcasm; Michael would see soon enough.

"Oh, the dead won't be much of a problem," Carson said, still grinning. "They are, in fact, all around us."

***

Carson was naked, sitting on the floor of the crematorium. The cement was cold on his bare skin, but he knew that this sensation wouldn't last long. He closed his eyes and took a deep breath in through his nose, before forcing it out again in a thin stream through his mouth.

It only took three of these breaths, of concentrating on his breath, of shutting his mind off, before his vision went dark.

And then he felt his mind flow like water being poured into a basin. In the dark void that encompassed him, he slowly picked out flecks of white, which quickly became a roiling, frothing sea.

Carson, so happy that you could make it back to me.

Leland Black stood on the beach, his black hat hiding his face. Holding his right hand was the little girl, the one that Leland said was the key to holding the rift open.

Amy.

The girl, like Leland, had her head hung low.

Carson wasn't sure if she could hear him, but the many times that he had transported his mind to the Marrow, she had never acknowledged him.

Have you found him yet? Have you found Robert?

Carson concentrated his thoughts.

No, we're looking—maybe you can help with that?

There was a pause.

I touched him—I can usually sense where he is, but...Robert is wandering, searching. His friends, on the other hand...they are back at the estate.

With the mention of the Harlop Estate, the fire in the sky roiled, and the face of James Harlop appeared in the flames.

And if you deal with his friends, he will come to you.

Thank you, Father.

Carson thought about that for a moment before continuing. Leland had helped him before, with the quiddity of the guard whose eyes he had torn out.

We need help...we need to speed them up, bring the dead forward.

To Carson's surprise, it wasn't Leland who replied, but the girl.

I can help with that, Amy said simply.

And then, without a moment's hesitation, Carson was transported back to the crematorium, his ass numb from the cold concrete.

When he opened his eyes, he was already smiling.

There were eleven people standing around him, their milky white eyes boring into him, awaiting instruction.

They were all dead.

***

"What the hell?" Michael whispered. Even Bella seemed surprised by the scene in the basement, despite how much Carson had shared with her over the years. Only Jonah seemed to be prepared for the scene, partly because he had been dealing with the dead for so many years now, whereas Michael and Bella's involvement usually ended with death. And mostly because of the woman in the oven, the one who had begged for him to come inside; there was that, too.

"Yes," Carson said, grinning widely. "Hell...hell is giving up your identity, of sacrificing the self. It may have been an evolutionary error, but now that it's here, it means everything."

Jonah gave him a strange look, but Carson ignored the short, fat man.

"These," Carson continued, gesturing to the eleven dead men and women that stood with their heads low as a show of obedience, "are what we will use to hold Robert's friends at bay, to lure him back to the estate."

Michael, still shirtless, his tattoos glistening with sweat from the hot crematorium basement, stepped onto the bottom rung and then reached for the closest quiddity. It was a woman dressed in a traditional pastel dress that ran to her ankles. Her blonde bangs hung over her eyes, but even through this, Carson could see the dark pits buried beneath. There was a nasty purple mark on her throat that descended into the neck of her dress, a wound that had been caked with layers of makeup.

"I wouldn't do that if I were you," Carson said calmly. Michael's hand hung in midair, only inches from the woman's head. "Remember what I told you, Michael, and you too, Jonah; you touch them, they send you to the Marrow."

Jonah looked up from his perch on the staircase.

"And?"

"And you don't come back…" Carson let his sentence trail off. "But there will be a time when we can all be free—free to come and go between worlds, to act and behave the way we see fit, not the way they want us to be."

Michael smiled, and Carson joined him. As Bella made her way down the stairs and passed both Jonah and the tattooed man to Carson, the eleven quiddity spread out, allowing her passage.

Carson couldn't help but think of himself as a king in that moment, with Bella as his queen. And these quiddity, they were his soldiers. Carson wrapped his arm around Bella's thin waist and pulled her tight.

"Jonah and Michael, I need you to go to the Harlop Estate. Use the dead to surround the place, to keep Robert's friends in order. I doubt Robert is there, but if he is, he needs to be re-strained. Whatever happens, do not let him touch one of the dead."

"Wait," Jonah interrupted, "why not? I thought you said—"

Carson shook his head.

"We need Robert—only Robert to open the rift in the Mar-row. I don't care what happens to the others."

When a smile crept on Jonah's wide face, revealing small, almost sinister teeth, Carson held up his hand.

"Before you get too excited, remember that we need his friends to draw Robert home."

Jonah stopped smiling.

"But, rest assured, when this is over, when the rift is opened back up, there will literally be hell on earth. And then you guys can go to work."

Michael spoke up next, in his usual monotone voice.

"What about them?" he asked, indicating the eleven men and women that still stood at the ready. "They gonna listen?"

Carson nodded.

"Oh, they'll listen all right."

"But how, why?"

Carson looked down at Bella, whose lips were pressed together tightly. He wondered what was going on in that mind of hers—she hadn't said much since coming downstairs and finding the dead standing there.

"Because when people die and don't go to the Marrow, they usually become confused, disoriented. Some don't even realize that they are dead. They need guidance, are looking for answers."

Bella looked up at him.

"You," she said, or asked; he couldn't tell if the word was a statement or a question based on her tone.

Carson shook his head.

"No, not me."

"Who, then?"

"Leland—Leland gave them the guidance they need."

At the mention of the man's name, several of the quiddity shifted, their first movement since allowing Bella to pass.

Carson smiled.

Even the dead feared the Goat.

That was good.

That was really good.

"Go on now, Jonah, Michael. Take these quiddity and let's have ourselves a party."

Chapter 13

"ANY TIME NOW," CAL grumbled, his eyes locked on the computer screen. After returning from the debacle at the cemetery, they had booted up Allan's laptop and were waiting patiently as he loaded the video from Seaforth. It took a couple of minutes of fast-forwarding through pitch blackness before the screen suddenly became awash in bright light. The image slowly dimmed, and then it transitioned into a strange gray color, as if someone had tried to be artistic and had applied an antique filter.

"Is it supposed to be this gray?" Shelly asked.

"No, not usually. But the camera was damaged in some way…normally, with the lens on, you can barely make out normal people."

Cal nodded, remembering the burnt-in image of Lorraine from the cemetery, while Walter had been just a silhouette.

"But for whatever reason, in the video you can make out Robert, and Sean, too. See there?"

Cal leaned in closer.

The image wasn't of great quality, but he could clearly see the outline of Robert's back as he walked ahead, Sean beside him, the latter holding his gun out at an angle. Cal cringed when the body of one of the hanged guards swayed in front of the lens, but Allan quickly moved the camera.

"Okay, so now what?" Shelly asked quietly. "What are we looking for? Why would you think that this whole camera thing in the cemetery would work?"

"Just watch."

The audio was likewise damaged—a dry hiss could be heard over their talking—but after twenty seconds or so, the sound of machine gun fire suddenly crackled from the laptop speakers.

There was a shout, too, something unintelligible, what Cal thought might have been his voice, and the camera whipped to one side. The image went squirrelly, scrambled lines scattering across the screen, but when Allan turned back again, it became relatively clear.

Except the scene wasn't the same. Instead of just Sean and Robert, the screen was filled with three glowing figures standing in front of Robert, while Sean was no longer in the frame.

"The dead guards," Cal said, more for himself than Allan or Shelly.

Robert was saying something on screen, but it was difficult to make out his exact words with all of the gunshots and shouts and the dry hiss that grated on Cal's nerves. But then Robert slowly and deliberately raised his hands out in front of him, and the words 'STOP' erupted from the speakers with unprecedented clarity.

"What is he—?" Shelly started, but Allan quickly hushed her.

What happened next was difficult to understand, despite the fact that Cal was watching it unfold before him. The glow from the three quiddity started to pixelate, and some of it, their hands, feet, the tops of their heads, started to extend out, stretching like computer-generated taffy.

And it was flowing toward Robert's hands.

Cal held his breath, knowing the consequences of being touched by the quiddity. As he watched, the glowing red and yellow hues started to stretch even further.

A split second before they touched Robert, however, the color built in front of his outstretched palms. And then it started to roil and froth, never quite making contact. The quiddity themselves lost some of their luster, leaving behind grayed-out shapes that were close, but not exactly, the same color as Robert's own outline.

"Jesus," Shelly whispered.

There was a flash of light in the center of Robert's chest, visible through his back, but the camera quickly panned away before Cal could see exactly what it was.

Several distinct gunshots could be heard next, and then Cal caught sight of his own image, his face a reflection of sheer terror, falling to the ground. He reached out frantically to stop his fall, but his hands only grasped a dead inmate, accidentally pulling him on top of him as they both went down.

And then there was a final gunshot, the report of which was unexpectedly cut off as the camera went black.

"What the fuck was that?" Shelly demanded. "What happened to Robert?"

Cal took a deep breath.

"Seriously. The, uh, the uh, oh what the fuck—that glowing shit, it went into Robert's hands?"

Allan shook his head.

"No, I don't think so, but it seemed like he could, I dunno, command it somehow. Pull it toward him. And you all saw what he did with the first guard, Quinn—how he seemed compelled to listen, to answer."

"But what was that in the center of his chest? The glow?"

"Dunno. Artifact, maybe."

Shelly, who was leaning on the back of Allan's chair, stood up straight, and the boy in the glasses bounced.

"I don't think so," she said softly. It was her tone that drew Cal's attention.

"You know something, don't you? Something you're not telling us?"

It wasn't meant as an accusation; he had intended it as more of an inquiry, but Shelly's expression immediately hardened. He wasn't even sure where it had come from. Still, as he waited for her to respond, he realized that it was something that had been bugging him for a while now. Shelly was so certain about specific things of which she should have no idea, an absolute confidence that exceeded even her typical attitude, that he was beginning to wonder if she really did know something that they didn't.

"No," she said at last. "But it was part of the tape. It was real. I felt—he told us that he felt pressure in his chest, remember? Whenever the quiddity are around?"

Cal didn't quite remember hearing anything about that, but he had also been buried beneath corpses, so it was possible. Or maybe he had said something in the chopper, but Cal was pretty fucked up then, too. They all were.

"Yeah, well, whatever it is, only he can do it," Cal said, averting his eyes. "Tried to tell Lorraine to stop in the cemetery. Even put my hands up like he did, and nada. Bitch kept walking."

Shelly scoffed at his crudeness.

"There's more," Allan informed them.

"More? More video?"

"No, not exactly. But I found some stuff online, about a book? Remember when Sean and Robert were talking about a book? With the prophecy about the Marrow? Well, as soon as we got back, I started searching the 'net. I didn't expect to find anything, because I've been searching for years about anything to do with the Marrow and I have never heard anything about it, but then…all of a sudden, about three and a half months ago, posts started popping up about *Inter vivos et mortuos*. Someone was suddenly on all the underground message board, asking questions about it. And then it stopped."

"Father Callahan," Cal said quickly. At nearly exactly the same time, Shelly said, "Robert."

Allan gave them both a strange look.

"Maybe, not sure—couldn't trace any of their IPs. I mean, if it were Callahan, it would explain why he was in the prison in the first place. But how would Robert know about the book?"

"Maybe his father told him," Shelly offered with a shrug.

Cal mulled this over, recalling the scars on Robert's calf. Something had happened in the Seventh Ward, something awful. And Cal was fairly certain that his friend's abrupt answers to his questions about what had happened were intentionally short.

He looked over at Shelly, who seemed lost in thought as well.

And she knows…she knows something. She knows a lot, maybe. More than she's letting on.

Shelly suddenly looked up, and Cal held her gaze in silence until she averted her eyes. And when the usually overconfident woman did that, Cal's suspicions were confirmed.

"I wish," Allan began, turning back to his computer. "I wish we just knew more, or if we had—"

But his sentence was cut short when the lights in the estate flickered.

"Forget to pay the power bill, Shel?"

When Shelly didn't answer, he looked over at her. She was clutching her chest, a pained expression on her pretty face.

"Someone's here," she said through clenched teeth. "Something is here."

Chapter 14

"ROBERT?" CAL ASKED, HIS voice tentative.

Shelly shook her head, her eyes wide, her hands still clasped against the center of her chest.

"Shel? What's wrong with you? You okay?"

Shelly shook her head again, and this time Cal went to her. Allan also stood, and was in the process of heading to her side, a concerned look on his face, when he stopped cold.

A heavy thumping on the door echoed into the family room.

Cal's heart skipped a beat.

"Jesus, Shel, what's going on?"

She still didn't answer, and her face started to turn a deep crimson. Cal grabbed her chin and raised her face to look directly into her eyes, his own heart beating through his chest.

The pounding on the door came again, but he ignored it.

"I'm—I'm okay," she wheezed at long last. She took a staggered breath, and her color started to return to close to normal.

"Who is it?" Cal asked, relief washing over him with the realization that she wasn't having a heart attack. "Who's at the door?" When Shelly just shook her head, he turned to Allan. "Go! Get her a glass of water!"

Allan, who was just staring at them, eyes wide behind the thick lenses, immediately bolted from the room.

The heavy knocking came again: bang, bang, bang.

"Fuck," Cal swore. He gently guided Shelly to the couch and laid her down. "Fucking hell, Shelly. Is it the door? Is it the person at the door?"

Shelly's face was pinched, and her skin was clammy to the touch.

"No," she managed, "Not person—persons."

"It's alright, it'll be alright. Is it your heart? You want an aspirin? What the fuck is happening?"

Shelly shook her head.

"Chest, so...tight..."

"Jesus Christ, what's going on?" he nearly shouted. Lifting his head, he yelled for Allan. "Allan! Get back here! Allan!"

But he heard nothing—Allan didn't respond. The knocking at the door seemed to have stopped as well.

"Allan?" he asked, his voice now tentative. "Where'd you go?"

He glanced down quickly to see that Shelly had closed her eyes, and then he looked back to the hallway that Allan had fled down only moments ago.

The silence in the Harlop Estate was alarming.

And frightening.

"Allan?"

Panic started to creep into Cal, and he gently patted Shelly's hand before rising to his feet. His eyes darted about the room, looking for anything that might be used as a weapon. Nothing jumped out at him. After what had happened with James Harlop, Robert had insisted that the fireplace utensils be removed. The only thing remotely close to a weapon were the cameras, tripods still attached, on the couch opposite Shelly where they had been lain after their encounter at the cemetery.

Cal swallowed hard.

It will have to do.

He grabbed the closest one, relishing the weight of it in his hand, and then he stepped out of the front sitting room.

The blood was instantly sucked from his face and limbs.

Allan was in the hallway, his glasses askew on his boyish face. His hair had been pulled back, thrusting his face upward. A short, four-inch blade glinted in the light.

The tip was pushed against the soft skin overlying his Adam's apple.

"Wha—?"

"Don't move," a nasally voice instructed.

Cal gulped and tilted his head ever so slightly to one side. The person standing behind Allan was shorter than him by about four or five inches, but his large belly could be seen on either side of Allan's thin frame. His face was hidden out of sight.

"Where's Robert?" the man hissed. When he spoke, his belly jiggled, and the blade skipped up and down ever so slightly against Allan's throat. Small dots of blood appeared where the tip touched his skin. "Where's Robert?"

"I—I don't know," Cal breathed. "Who are you? What do you want?"

"Robert—I want Robert! Where is he!" As the man shouted, he shoved Allan forward, moving with him, somehow managing to keep the knife in place despite their awkward dance.

Cal was so taken aback by the sudden movement that he stumbled backward. His legs were numb, and he nearly fell with the first step. Righting himself by holding his hands out for balance, he realized that he was still holding the camera.

Without thinking, he raised the lens and then started clicking away, much like he had back in the cemetery. When the two kept moving forward, backing Cal into the sitting room, a sinking feeling came over him.

Whoever the man with the knife was, he was alive.

"Where is he?" the man bellowed.

"I don't know! He—he left!"

Allan was crying now, tears streaming down his frightened face.

"Please," he begged, but the man, who Cal realized now was pulling his hair from behind, told him to shut up.

"Who are you?" Cal asked.

"Never mind who the fuck I am—you best be thinking of how to find Robert!"

Find him? Who is this psychopath? And what does he want with Robert?

Cal lowered the camera, his mind working a mile a minute, desperately trying to come up with a way to save his friend's life. It seemed ludicrous that despite what they had been through together at Seaforth, now Alan was going to meet his end at the hands of a mere mortal.

A short, squat human with a deviated septum.

It was unfathomable.

"Nah, nah, I don't think so," a female voice suddenly said. "I think you best be figuring out a way to stop your head from bleeding."

Shelly seemed to materialize out of thin air; at some point during the man's rush toward Cal, she must have used this as a distraction and had risen from the couch.

Now she was standing just inside the entrance to the room, just as Allan was shoved over the threshold. In response to her threat, the man made a strange growling noise and turned, still clutching a fistful of Allan's hair.

Shelly swung the camera tripod with vicious intent. A resounding crack filled the Harlop sitting room when the metal legs collided with the top of the man's bald head. Cal gasped, but he wasn't terribly surprised; he had seen her in action before, back in the Seventh Ward, and he knew just how violent and ruthless Shelly could be.

The man dropped like a stone, his hands releasing the knife and Allan's hair. He hit the ground even before the geyser of blood landed.

Allan fell forward onto his knees, coughing as he scrambled like a baby just learning to crawl, until he was right up next to Cal.

"You think you can come in here with a fucking pen knife and threaten us?" Shelly shouted at the man who was rolling on the ground, his head and face cupped in his chubby hands. She reared back, intent on swinging the now dented tripod again—one of the legs was dangling, twisted—but then something gave her pause.

The man on the ground wasn't gasping or sobbing, as Cal had first thought. As he watched, he pulled his hands away from his face, revealing blood from a wound on the top of his head that had trickled down into his mouth, speckling his teeth with red stains.

He wasn't even groaning.

He was laughing.

"Why the fuck are you laughing?" Shelly demanded, stepping even closer to the man, making sure he could see the tripod she was brandishing.

The man only continued to laugh in her face. Cal watched on in horror, unable to react. Shelly gritted her teeth and swung the tripod down on his massive gut this time, and the man's short legs immediately shot up. He coughed and his hands went to the point of impact, but then he started laughing even harder. Blood that had dripped into his mouth was spraying from his thin lips, only to land on his face moments later.

The tripod was completely smashed, all three legs broken into three jagged spears.

"Tell me why you're laughing," Shelly demanded, her pale face twisted into a scowl. "Or I'll stab you in your fucking guts."

Allan made his way to his feet, and he cowered behind Cal.

The man finally stopped laughing.

"Because," he gasped, still out of breath from either the blows or the laughing, or both. "Because I didn't come alone, you idiot."

Cal, who had been slowly sidling toward the knife that was now only a few feet from him, froze.

"What?" Shelly asked, her posture becoming defensive.

"I didn't come alone," he repeated. He brought two fingers to his lips and whistled, spraying blood all over his hand and the hardwood below. Shelly took a step backward, and Cal reached down and snatched up the blade.

It had looked massive, like a machete, when it was pressed against Allan's throat, but now that it was in his hand, it felt as puny as a Swiss army knife.

"I brought some friends," the fat man whispered as he grunted and pushed himself to his knees.

There was a rustling sound from behind Cal, and he whipped around. The knife clanged to the floor.

"No," he moaned.

Three people approached, their heads low, their complexion gray, indistinct. He couldn't see their eyes, but he didn't have to to know that they were dark black orbs.

They were dead.

Cal heard Shelly scream, and he turned back the other way so quickly that he felt sick.

There were dead people everywhere, all shuffling toward Cal, Shelly, and Allan, encircling them.

And through their heavy breathing and shuffling steps, Cal could make out the wet sound of the fat man's nasally laugh.

PART II - *Inter vivos et*

mortuos

Chapter 15

ROBERT WATTS STARTED LOOKING in the only place he could think of: Father Callahan's church. And, surprisingly, it hadn't been all that difficult to find.

His memories, the ones that Sean Sommers had forced him to recall, ones that he hadn't even been aware of before having met the man, had given him some clues. And he found that the more he concentrated, the deeper he went into his own mind and the more he remembered.

It was a small church with a high-peaked roof located some-where warm—in the South. It had massive wooden doors that swung inward, not all that much unlike the Harlop Estate. But other than the stately doors, it was otherwise a fairly plain and modest structure.

Noise.

He remembered constant noise, as if there was construction going on around the church.

Robert could have tried to reach out to Sean, as he was pos-itive that he knew where the church was, but that was the last thing he wanted to do. Sean Sommers wasn't who Robert had thought he was.

The man had shot and killed someone in cold blood, a man who had his hands bound behind his back, no less. And he had also pushed the Seaforth warden into the Marrow, which might have even been worse. No, the last thing he wanted was Sean Sommers knowing where he was going.

Or why.

In fact, Robert wanted nothing to do with the man ever—irrespective of the fact that they were both Guardians of the Marrow, and their fates seemed intrinsically bound.

And then there was the whole issue of Carson, of his brother...Robert just hadn't been able to bring himself to kill the man, despite knowing that it was the right thing to do. That it would be in the best interest of everyone, living and dead, that it would even be merciful.

But he couldn't do it.

And yet he *had* killed.

Just thinking about firing the pistol at Father Callahan caused a knot to form in his stomach so tight that it nearly made him sick.

It was the only way, Robert—the only way.

Maybe, but he had still taken a man's life.

Robert opened the window to his rented Chevy and let the hot air slap him in the face. As the wind accosted him, he closed his eyes for a brief moment.

But then they quickly snapped open again.

It wasn't just because he was driving, but more because every time he closed his eyes, blackness overcame him, an all-encompassing void that would eventually crystallize and become a sea.

And then his mind would be back with Leland on the shores of the Marrow. And he wasn't ready to go back. Not yet, at least.

Less than an hour later of uneventful driving, Robert found himself outside the South Carolina Public Records in Columbia.

He wasn't completely sure why he was there—he definitely hadn't consciously decided to drive to South Carolina—but it just felt *right*, and like when he had ordered the quiddity at Seaforth to stop, it just felt natural, normal, *right*.

Robert shut off the car and took a deep breath before opening the door. He pulled the cheap sunglasses he had bought at a gas station down to cover the dark circles around his eyes, and then quickly made his way across the street.

The place was deserted, which wasn't entirely surprisingly given that it was 2 p.m. on a Tuesday. His objective was to find the church, find the book, and then see what was so important in it that Father Callahan would use his final words before begging to be killed instructing him to find it.

And then he would get the fuck out of South Carolina, hopefully without raising suspicion, without keying Sean in to the fact that he was looking for the book.

Robert approached the large front doors to the building, grabbed the handle, then put on his best fake smile before pulling it wide. Cold air blasted him in the face, immediately drying the sweat on his forehead. Allowing his eyes to adjust to the dim lighting, Robert stood in the entrance for a moment. When he began to make out the outline of a desk just ten paces inside the door, he started toward it.

A thin woman with prominent eyebrows sat behind the desk. She had a book in her lap and her eyes were focused on the pages. Robert leaned over the desk and took a look. He caught the title, but not the author: *Bad Games*.

"Whatcha reading?" he asked softly.

The woman jumped.

"Woah! You scared me."

Robert took a step backward, scolding himself for being too casual.

You're trying to find out about the church, not get a date.

Thoughts of Shelly came flooding in, but he forced them away. It wasn't fair what he'd done, leaving both Cal and Shelly in the dark, but it was *less* fair bringing them on for a ride. He was done with that life, done with getting them involved. Irrespective of what Cal said, it *was* about him—him and Amy.

And they didn't deserve to be pulled down into the depths with him.

"Sorry," he said sheepishly. "I didn't mean to frighten you."

The woman swallowed hard and adjusted her glasses that had shifted when she was startled.

"Fine, fine," she said dismissively. "What can I do ya for?"

"I'm looking for something…I mean, someone. Well, not them, exactly, but where they might live, where their next of kin is."

The woman scrunched her forehead suspiciously, making her eyebrows join into one large, thick caterpillar.

"Excuse me?"

Robert pulled his sunglasses off and sighed.

"Look, a friend of mine passed away, and I'm looking to find his next of kin to inform them."

The woman chewed the inside of her lip.

"Your friend died, but you don't know where he lives? Where his family lives?"

Robert looked away, trying not to smile. It was going exactly as he had imagined, minus the first part, but he attributed her jumpiness to *Bad Games* and not his own actions. He looked back at the secretary, this time getting serious.

"He was a priest—my sponsor," he said quietly, looking around dramatically to make sure that nobody was listening.

"Sponsor?"

Robert leaned in even closer.

"Twelve steps."

The woman's mouth and eyes formed the exact same shape: wide and circular.

"Oh, I see," she said after an awkward pause. Now it was her time to lean in. "What's his name? Let me see if I can help you out. A priest, you said? From SC?"

Robert nodded slowly.

"Yeah," he replied dryly, "a priest."

He waited for the woman to turn to her monitor and start typing away.

"Okay, I think I can help you out—if your friend owned the church, that is. Or his house, that's all part of the public record. We normally defer this kind of thing to the local agencies, but for priests...what's his name?"

"Callahan."

The woman looked up at him.

"Is that his first or last name?"

"Last."

"And what is his first name?"

"Father?"

"Seriously?"

Robert shook his head.

"Look, I don't know. I only knew him as Father Callahan—sponsors, well, they aren't supposed to get too personal." Robert scratched his neck. "And, to be honest with you, ma'am, I'm not the, uh, the best student, if you know what I mean."

The woman blinked hard and then nodded.

"Father Callahan it is."

Then she went back to typing.

"You know him?"

Her eyes still glued to her computer, she punched a few keys and then the printer behind her starting whirring.

"No, it's just that you are the second person this week to ask for Father Callahan's church address. Must have been a popular sponsor, don't you think? It pains me to think that he is dead, though. At least—at least he made a difference in someone's life."

Robert's mouth fell open.

It couldn't be a coincidence. Someone else was also looking for *Inter vivos et mortuos*.

The secretary grabbed the paper from the printer and turned back to him. Before she could even raise her gaze from the page, Robert snatched it from her hand.

"Yeah, he must have been," he said absently. Then he started to walk away, staring at the address on the page, one that looked strangely familiar.

"Good luck with your recovery," the woman whispered after him.

Robert didn't turn back. If someone else was looking for the book, then they were probably looking for him as well.

He picked up his pace and left the church.

Chapter 16

IT WASN'T EXACTLY THE way Robert remembered it, but pretty damn close. Father Callahan's parish was a simple structure, and years of being in the sun and not properly cared for had taken their toll on the exterior. Only the impressive front doors, the ones that all those years ago he had stood in front of hand in hand with Sean, looked like they were in decent shape. The obnoxious construction that he remembered from his time here had long since passed. In fact, it looked like the entire area had gone through several life cycles. Once located at the end of a cul-de-sac surrounded by manufacturing buildings, the church now stood like a spire in the center of a derelict wasteland of abandoned buildings, a consequence of America's outsourcing.

Robert started breathing heavily the moment he opened his car door, and the anxiety continued to build with every step that he took. He was on the verge of hyperventilating by the time he walked up to the giant wooden doors.

Please, take the boys…I can only take one…that one…

In the back of his mind, Robert wondered if Carson was right, if things would have been different if it had been his brother that Callahan had taken in and not him.

Of course it would be different…but you wouldn't become Carson. You are a good person.

Robert tried to push the thoughts from his mind, but they persisted. So instead of denying them, he attacked their validity instead.

How do you even know that that actually happened? That Sean coming here with you and Carson was real?

Part of him thought, hoped, even, that these memories were somehow just planted in his head by Sean, a way of getting him to do his bidding…

But that brought about other questions, ones that sent him skipping down the rabbit hole.

What, exactly did Sean want him to do? What was his diabolical master plan?

Robert shook his head.

It didn't really matter what Sean wanted, or what the man was trying to accomplish. What mattered was getting Amy back, and making sure that the Marrow stayed the way it was — closed up tight.

That evil was confined to the flames above the sea.

And then he came full circle to the reason why he was standing outside the dead priest's church, wearing baggy jeans and oversized sunglasses: the book. It was a stretch, he knew, but he hoped that *Inter vivos et mortuos* would shed some light on his purpose.

For some reason, Robert knocked on the heavy wooden doors, even though he wasn't sure who he expected to answer. He waited for several seconds out of respect, but when the only response was only silence from within, he grabbed the wooden handle and pulled.

Half of him expected the church to be locked, what with Father Callahan having been dead and gone for nearly three months now. But it was a church, after all, and these things had a penchant for remaining open, even though all rational thought suggested that they should be boarded up forever.

The door opened, and Robert squinted into the darkness, his pupils trying to adjust to the dramatic contrast in light.

And then he stepped inside.

There were several lit candles on a table off to one side, which either meant they were burning infernal, or there were still parishioners who visited despite the old priest's passing. He would have put his money on the latter.

"Hello?" he said gently. Again, not surprisingly, no one answered.

The door closed behind him, and then Robert was left with only the candles to light his way. The church was modest, the pews in the same general state of disrepair as the exterior of the church. As his eyes continued to adjust, he realized that he wasn't as alone as he had first thought. He made out the outline of four heads, all bowed, scattered throughout the pews.

And of course there was also Jesus; the man was hanging on a cross high above the altar, the candlelight reflecting off his plastic face, making him look eerily like the faces in the flames above the Marrow.

A chill suddenly raced up and down Robert's spine, causing him to shudder. A memory came rushing back with such force that he had to brace himself against the back of a pew to avoid toppling.

"Come with me, son," Father Callahan said as he took Robert's small hand in his.

Robert hesitated and he looked up at the man, confused as to what was happening. The man who called himself Sean had come to get him and his brother at home, telling him that his father had been in an accident. That they had to go with him to find a new home.

But now they were separating, and Robert felt a tightness in his chest.

This wasn't supposed to happen — none of this was supposed to happen.

He turned and watched as Sean walked away from the church, still holding Carter's hand. His brother never turned back, and Robert started to cry.

"It's okay, son. You are safe here. Please," Callahan said as he opened the door with a grunt, "there is someone I want you to meet."

Robert sniffed, then wiped the tears away with the sleeve of his shirt.

Daddy didn't like it when he cried; he was a big boy now, he had to be tough, strong.

With a deep breath, Robert followed the priest inside the church.

"Kendra!" Father Callahan shouted, and a little girl of about seven or eight, several years older than Robert himself, appeared seemingly out of nowhere, her messy blonde hair hanging in front of her face.

"Robert, I want you to meet Kendra. You two can be friends."

Robert coughed, then blinked, trying to force feeling back into his legs.

What the hell was that?

He coughed again, a hacking cough that brought up some phlegm, then felt a pang of pain in the back of his calf.

Biting his tongue to avoid crying out, he grabbed the area and rubbed it until the skin beneath his jeans turned red. Then he stood and stretched his back, and tried to catch his bearings.

Memories or visions or hallucinations or not, he was here to find the book. And the fact that his leg was hurting meant that he had to hurry. Things were happening again, and he didn't have much time before…before what?

He didn't know for certain. But something told him that the pain in his leg was like the pain in his chest when the quiddity were near; only with his leg, it was something worse.

It was Leland reaching out to him.

The Goat is your father, Robert.

Grimacing, he took a step forward, his eyes scanning the interior of the church that still seemed foreign to him even though he was beginning to suspect that he had, in fact, been here before.

The book, I need to find the book.

Moving deeper into the church, he felt sweat begin to bead on his forehead.

I need to find Inter vivos et mortuos. *It's the only way I will get Amy back.*

Chapter 17

IT WAS CLEAR THAT someone had been to the church before Robert, searching for something—most likely either himself, or the book. The lady at the records building hadn't been mistaken.

It wasn't so much the fact that some of the dust on the table with the candles had been disturbed, or that the cabinets in the small office of the church had recently been opened and closed, that tipped him off, but that there had been an obvious effort to put things back the way they had been—*exactly* how they had been.

As Robert looked about the church, trying to fit in with the other doting parishioners, he realized that it wasn't something that Father would have left in the open. If it had been, then whoever was here before would have found it, which was still a distinct possibility.

An image of Callahan's mouth, twisted in sheer agony, mouthing the words, '*the book, go find the book*,' flashed in his mind.

If it's not here, where am I supposed to look, then? It must be in a location only I would be able to find…

Robert stood alone in the small office, breathing deeply, trying to remain calm and still his frazzled nerves. Part of him wanted to just forget about this whole ordeal, pack up, and head to Canada as he had once considered doing with Amy.

Amy…

But it was Amy that kept him going.

Robert shook his head, then made his way back into the main section of the church, all the while mumbling to himself.

"Think, Robert. Think…Father Callahan wanted you to find the book, and the only logical place to look is here, in his church, the church that you were dropped off at. He would have put it somewhere where only you could find it."

His frustration mounting, Robert decided that instead of rifling through the dead priest's belongings, as someone likely more experienced than he had already done, he would take a different approach.

He would look inward for answers.

Robert hadn't barely been able to close his eyes since being touched by Leland without feeling that darkness, the threat of his mind being transported to the Marrow, but he was running thin on options.

Determined now, he slowly made his way to the front of the church, and took a seat on the first pew. It had been a long time since he had been in a church, and longer still since he had sat in a pew as a common parishioner. But it felt oddly comfortable and familiar to him.

Then he closed his eyes, relaxed his neck and shoulders, and took a deep breath.

Think, Robert. Think back to before…

"You coming? If you're hiding with me, you better hurry; she's almost done counting."

Robert looked at Kendra, a smile on his young face.

"She's too slow, you know she never finds us."

Kendra reached out and grabbed his arm and tugged.

"Come on, I have something I want to show you anyway."

Robert reluctantly went with her, allowing himself to be pulled from the back room with their beds to the front of the church.

It was a Thursday afternoon, a sweltering, sunny afternoon, which was pretty much the only weather that South Carolina had this time of year, and stepping from the cool, air conditioned sleeping quarters into the warm, humid church was a shock to his system.

If God is so almighty and powerful, then why doesn't he cool his own house?

Still, the weather had done nothing to keep the devotees away.

There was an elderly woman hovering by the candles at the side of the church dressed in black, her head hung low. There was another person, a middle-aged man, on his knees in the middle pew, his lips moving in silent prayer.

And then there was Father Callahan, his face twisted in a frown as he spoke to a third parishioner by the front, his long, flowing robes somehow pristine despite the heat.

"C'mon!" Kendra hissed, tugging him even harder. She was guiding him toward the altar, which Callahan had told them repeatedly was a definite no-no.

But Kendra, she just had this way about her, one that made it near impossible for him to resist her games that would inevitably result in at least a strong scolding.

Robert stole another glance over his shoulder at the priest, trying to move quietly, to not draw his attention. Kendra, on the other hand, moved like an elephant, and he cringed when she literally jumped onto the platform and landed hard with two feet. Robert followed quickly, his eyes still aimed toward the front of the church.

What few people realized about the church was that the heavy curtain that hung down from the ceiling behind the altar wasn't there to cover an unsightly wall, or an exit door. If you paid enough attention, you could see it flutter occasionally, revealing the fact that there was air behind it.

Most people were too wrapped up in their own heads to notice, and the few that did probably didn't care. But to Kendra, it was an adventure, a secret in the waiting.

Kendra snaked her way against the sidewall, and then reached out to tease the curtain back. Then she turned back to face Robert.

"Come on," she said, her eyes wild, her smile bright. "Christine will never find us in here."

Robert grimaced, knowing that if the altar was off limits, then this area, the sanctum that Father Callahan was so secretive about, was *definitely* an area that they were forbidden to enter.

But Kendra pulled, and Robert was literally yanked behind the curtain. At the last second, however, he whipped his head around.

Father Callahan was staring at him, a scowl etched on his face.

Then the curtain flipped closed behind them. A second later, it came to rest, and it was as if they were never there.

Robert slowly opened his eyes, his breathing still slow and regular. As he waited to recover from the vivid memory, his gaze began to focus on the dark red curtain at the back of the altar. In his vision, it had been a plush, bright crimson, but today, it was a dull red, pilly and neglected.

But it was the same curtain nonetheless.

Robert knew where Father Callahan had kept the book. He had known it all along.

Chapter 18

A QUICK GLANCE REVEALED that the church's few parishioners were predictably too engrossed in their own heads to even acknowledge him.

Robert teased the curtain back and peered behind. The space was much like he remembered it: a rectangular area about five feet deep that ran the length of the altar. There was a folding table on the side opposite where Robert had entered, upon which sat a box of wafers and several half-empty bottles of wine for Mass.

Robert strode over to the table with a purpose, but as he approached, his heart began to sink.

Like the files in Callahan's office, the candles out front, it was clear that the people that had searched the church before him had come back here, too.

"Shit," he murmured. He was coming to the realization that not only was it possible that the people who had been here before had found the book, but that it was almost a given.

Whoever *they* were.

As Robert picked up the wafers, he scolded himself for being so stupid.

You thought that you would just saunter up to the church and the book would just be sitting on the desk for you? Maybe with a giant beacon of light illuminating it from the sky above?

He tossed the wafers back on the table, his eyes focusing on the wine. It didn't seem like a half-bad idea. But as Robert reached for one of the bottles, he noticed a small Post-it note beneath where the wafers had lay.

As soon as he picked it up, he knew that it was meant for him despite the lack of salutation.

It was just one sentence, scrawled in crooked handwriting; Father Callahan's hand:

Hide-and-seek.

The memory came like a lightning bolt in his brain.

"No, not just behind here," Kendra said, "but in here!"
Robert looked at the wild girl before him, and grimaced.
"Where? I don't see—"
Kendra pushed the wall, and he heard a click and then a secret door, only about three feet tall, popped open.
Robert's eyes bulged.
"What? How?"
Kendra giggled and shook her head.
"Just get in—quick, before Christine comes!"
Before Robert could say differently, before he started to complain, to tell Kendra that, 'Oh, I don't know, this seems like a bad idea, Father Callahan won't be happy,' he was yanked inside a tiny, hidden room that reeked of soot and flame.

Robert blinked, and his gaze immediately went to the spot on the opposite wall. Like back then, he couldn't see what Kendra had; the plaster wall looked just like a plain old wall. Sure, it was in dire need of some cosmetic repair, but there was no hint of a secret door.

"It *must* be in there."

When Father Callahan had seen them head behind the curtain all those years ago, he must have known that Kendra would have found the secret room.

His gaze darted to the sticky note once more.

Hide-and-seek.

Robert immediately went to a spot on the wall that seemed familiar, and pushed, his heart racing.

Nothing happened; he felt only plaster beneath his hand.

There was no click, no give even.

Robert moved his hand a little lower and to the left, and pushed again.

Nothing.

Frowning, he took a step backward and examined the wall for a seam or maybe a shadow. The problem was that the plaster was so old and badly damaged that there were seams *everywhere*. There could have been a thousand secret doors, or none at all.

One vertical line in particular looked promising, and he pressed just below it.

Still nothing.

His frustration was starting to mount, along with skepticism.

Was that a real memory? How come I know nothing else about this girl? About Kendra? Who is she? Where is she?

Robert couldn't help but think that maybe these memories or visions or whatever the hell they were were simply some sort of idea that Sean had somehow injected into his mind.

After all, it had been at the Harlop Estate with Sean that he had had his first memory, that time of being dropped off at the church. It had also been under Sean's encouragement, his guidance.

Maybe he hypnotized me?

Robert shook his head.

I don't remember—why *don't I remember?*

He could vividly remember his father and mother, Alex and Helen Watts, a litigator and a homemaker, and he could even remember the house he grew up in. True, he couldn't remember much before he was six years old, but who did? His memory of his grandfather was equally vivid, especially the way the man always smelled of cigars and how he had taught Robert how to cut his own.

He couldn't remember anything about his supposed brother, Carson, or Leland, or…his real mother? She had never appeared in his visions.

At least not yet.

Robert pushed the wall again, this time with the heel of his hand hard enough to make him wince.

Visions, memories, the Marrow.

For what felt like the hundredth time, Robert thought that all this time he was either hallucinating, or that he was actually dead already.

"Where the hell are you?" he grumbled.

As he systematically moved a foot to his right and prepared himself to slam his hand against the wall like an idiot again, a sudden commotion from the other side of the curtain stopped him cold.

"Alright, everyone out—church is gonna be closed for an hour or two," a man said from out front. The voice was muffled from behind the thick curtain, but it sounded familiar to him nonetheless.

"Ma'am? I'm sorry but you're going to have to leave. Just for an hour or so, then you can come back in."

Robert heard a woman protest, but the man was persistent.

The church is closed?

Heart racing, Robert waited silently for what felt like an hour. Finally, he heard the front door click closed, and then another person spoke up.

"Clear. Why we here, anyway? We searched the church already."

There was a short pause. And when the first man replied, he sounded much closer than he had before.

"Boss told us to search again. He wants the book."

Boss...

Robert's eyes bulged.

Aiden!

It was the man from the helicopter, from Seaforth. The one with the chewing tobacco jammed in his lip, who had helped him and Sean survive the mess hall disaster.

And they're looking for the book...on Sean's orders.

Robert whipped his head around and began using both hands now to press the wall, desperately trying to find the door.

The last thing he wanted was to be caught here by those men.

Sean had permitted him to leave the helicopter, but he wasn't so certain that if they crossed paths again, that he would be so eager. And Robert hadn't forgotten that they had been in the process of flying away when he had stumbled out of the prison.

"A book? This is all about a book?"

Robert kept pushing the wall, sweat dripping into his eyes.

Where the fuck is it...where the fuck is it...c'mon, open the fuck up!

"A book," Aiden confirmed, his voice directly on the other side of the curtain now. "But you know what he said to do if we come across Robert."

"Ten four."

At the sound of his name, Robert became even more frantic. He glanced over his shoulder while he pressed randomly on the wall, and caught sight of a hand grip the edge of the curtain, less than ten feet from where he stood.

"What's with this book, anyway?"

"You ask too many questions, you know that, Mark?"

And then Robert heard a muted click.

Yes!

The secret door popped open, the same size and shape as in his memory. Robert yanked it open and, without even looking, he jumped inside and pulled it closed behind him.

"Just a curious fella, I guess," Mark said a split second before the curtain was yanked back.

Chapter 19

ROBERT WAITED IN COMPLETE darkness for what felt like several hours. He heard the men outside the secret passage rifling through the late Father Callahan's items and stomping around just inches from where he sat. Even after they had receded into the main church area, their voices far too muffled behind the hidden door to make out anything specific, he waited.

And then he waited some more.

And some more.

Only after what felt like several hours did Robert dare pull from his pocket the burner cell phone he had picked up at the same time as the sunglasses and check the time. It read 2:20. He hadn't checked the time when he had arrived, but he knew that he had left the records building around 12:20, so guesstimating a twenty-minute drive to the church, ten more minutes fucking around without finding the passage, and all told it meant that he had been cramped in the hidden room for an hour and a half.

His legs ached and his back throbbed, the latter necessarily crooked to allow him to fit in the small space. Although he didn't remember much of the time that he and Kendra had hidden in here, it was obviously much more comfortable back then, as both of them had fit. As it was, something hard poked into his hip, and there was what he presumed was a shelf poking into the back of his head.

And it reeked of soot.

Robert shut off the cell phone and waited.

And waited.

He had seen Aiden at Seaforth; he knew the man to be calculating, precise, no nonsense, unfazed by the horrors around him. So even when it felt like his whole body had become numb from being half seated, half crouched for hours, Robert remained still and silent.

When he turned his phone on again, it was nearly four o'clock. Only then, after not hearing a sound for a long, long time, did Robert dare use his phone's flashlight. He was almost positive that no light could eke out from the hidden door, but it wasn't worth the risk—until now, when he was absolutely certain that the men were gone.

The room was even smaller than he'd thought, and he immediately experienced a psychosomatic response to the confined quarters. He wasn't typically claustrophobic, but his muscles ached, and seeing that he was crammed in a space that couldn't have been much larger than a square foot, made his muscles seize as if racked with tetanus.

The passage extended upward, beyond the reaches of the weak light from his cheap cell phone. The thing digging into his head was indeed a shelf as he had first thought, but it was empty. He tried to turn around, but could only manage to get halfway before another shelf jammed into the soft tissue between his ribs. Instead, Robert reached behind him and grabbed the thing that was poking into his back.

His initial response was one of frustration; it wasn't *the* book—it wasn't *Inter vivos et mortuos*. Instead of an ancient text, the dark navy cover felt like plastic, as if it had been purchased from a drug store.

When Robert opened the first page, he realized that it was a photo album. Interest piqued, he held the flashlight to the black-and-white photograph.

It was a much younger Father Callahan and a man who looked a lot like Sean Sommers with his arm around his shoulders. In fact, it looked too much like Sean as Robert knew him now. Father Callahan, on the other hand, looked some thirty years younger, and the quality of the photograph suggested that it was at least that old.

But it certainly *looked* like Sean—the same stern expression, the same square haircut, a cigarette dangling from his lips.

His father, maybe?

Robert was in the process of flipping to the next page when he felt a bolt of anxiety.

Not here for a trip down memory lane—you never know when they might come back. Focus, Robert. Focus.

He was here to find the book.

He was here for *Inter vivos et mortuos.*

Robert closed the album and held it in one hand, while at the same time splaying the cell phone light on the other shelves. The photo album was the only thing on the lowest level, and as he moved the cell phone upward, he realized that it was the only thing on *any* level, at least as far as he could see.

On a whim, he reached up with his left hand and felt around the shelf just above his head. The only thing he got for his trouble was a face full of dust. On instinct, he inhaled, and then stifled a cough as the dust coated the inside of his nose and sinuses.

"It has to be here," he whispered after successfully forcing the cough away.

Hide-and-seek.

Robert sighed and rolled his neck, trying to work out a crick. As he did, he stared upward into the darkness. For a moment, he said and did nothing, but with the flashlight now pressed against his jeans, face down, his eyes slowly became accustomed to the pervasive darkness. And there, about fourteen or fifteen feet up, he thought he caught sight of something protruding from a shelf. Something that *could* be the corner of a book.

It could also just be a defect in the shelf itself. The ones on the lower levels were the shitty particle board kind, and he wasn't at all sure why Father Callahan had installed them in the first place.

Or why he would build them so high.

Still…

Robert squinted harder, straining to make out more of the shape.

Failing to identify anything else, he brought the light up again, but when this only served to blind him, he gave up trying to figure out what it was.

At least from a seated position.

Stretching and straining his leg muscles, Robert somehow managed to rise. With a groan, he tried his best to hyperextend his back, to work out the knots that had formed over the afternoon.

To his dismay, he still couldn't tell what the object was even when standing.

There's only one way to find out if it's the book.

Without thinking, Robert jammed the photo album into the back of his pants. Then, after reaching upward and confirming the solidity of the shelves, he started to climb.

Twice Robert panicked, thinking that the shelves were going to give way. But while they flexed and bent, they somehow managed to hold. He systematically went up, putting the cell phone on the next shelf as he moved up a rung.

And when his feet rested on the fourth or fifth shelf, he had made it to the object in the dark.

Shifting the cell phone onto that shelf, which was now at eye level, Robert squinted and waited for his pupils to dilate.

And when they did, a sigh of relief passed over him.

It *was* a book; a book with a thick leather cover coated in dust. Without thinking, Robert blew on it and the air instantly became thick with soot. He tried his best to stifle his cough, as he had done before, but the dust motes, thick as pregnant beetles, caught in his throat and he was overcome. His body shuddered with the intensity of the cough, so much so that he nearly lost his footing.

His reaction was so visceral that he dry heaved from it, all the while blood pulsed in his ears like an ocean reminiscent of the Marrow.

When he finally managed a deep, hitching breath, he heard the voices. They were still muffled, but their shouts were close and distinct enough for him to make out the words.

Aiden and the other man, Mark, hadn't left the church after all.

He pictured the man with the chewing tobacco jammed in his lip, the automatic weapon resting against his shoulder.

I should have known.

"...in the walls...he's in the walls...find the door..."

Robert's pulse was pounding so hard that his entire body rocked. He let go of the book and flooded the light from the cell phone upward.

He coughed again, and in between heaves, he could hear someone pounding on the wall somewhere below him.

Robert slipped the cell phone between his teeth, grabbed the book in one hand, and did the only thing that he could think of.

He went up.

Chapter 20

ROBERT'S ARMS WERE BURNING, and the thick layer of dust that coated his mouth and throat made it difficult to breath.

And yet upward he climbed. The shelves had since given way to simple bricks jutting from the walls, and they had become progressively grimier on the way up. The soldiers continued to thump on the walls below, desperately trying to find a way in. Eventually, they would find the opening, but he was more concerned with the fact that they might just get bored and begin firing into the walls instead.

After all, Robert had the book and, for what it was worth, he had the photo album, but neither of these would do him any good if he was dead.

Robert pulled himself up another foot, trying, and failing, to do some mental gymnastics to figure out how much higher he had to go before he reached the top of the church. He wouldn't even allow himself to consider the possibility that there wasn't a way out up top.

One more rung, and the crown of his head struck something solid, causing his teeth to snap down on the tip of his tongue. Pain radiated from the point of impact, but he fought the urge to cry out. Unlike the coughing fit that had given him away the first time, this time he won the battle. Delicately balancing the book on a jutting brick, and with the cell phone now clenched between his teeth, Robert used both hands to push up.

Nothing happened—it was just like pushing against the wall below.

Robert forced the pain in his arms and legs away and pushed upward with all of his might. Just as he ran out of strength, he felt something give—just a little, but enough to fuel his hope.

He relaxed his arms again, reset his feet, then took a deep breath. Just as he reached the end of his exhalation, he heard a sickening sound from somewhere far below him.

It was a metallic click; the sound of the door being opened.

Robert's eyes bulged, and he quickly shoved upward with both hands, his triceps and calves screaming with the effort. No longer worried about the noise, he grunted and gasped as he strained.

"Found the door! Aiden, I found the door!"

Light spilled into the shaft from below, and just as he heard the much larger man finagling his way inside, he shoved upward again.

There was a tearing sound, like a rug being separated by its very fibers, and Robert suddenly found himself squinting from light that spilled in through the crack. The contrast between the chimney illuminated by only his cell phone and the bright mid-afternoon South Carolina sun was so dramatic that for a second, he felt paralyzed.

A shot rang out, and something whizzed by his ear, sending pain flaring on that side of his head. Bright light or not, Robert pushed again, and a square foot of plywood suddenly came loose. He shoved it aside, and it careened out of sight. As Robert hoisted himself out of the tunnel and onto the roof, he heard Mark shout from below.

"He's on the roof! Aiden, he's on the roof!"

In his haste, Robert nearly propelled himself too far, and he had to reach back and desperately grab the lip of what he now saw was the top of a chimney in order to prevent from sliding down the sloped roof.

"Fuck!" he groaned, every muscle in his body crying out in protest.

As he hung there, trying to coax his muscles into responding and trying to decide what to do next, he finally got a good look at himself.

His hands and arms were completely black, covered in a thick layer of soot. His shirt was likewise a dark mess. Clearly, when Father Callahan had closed off the fireplace and turned it into a secret room, he hadn't bothered cleaning it all the way to the top.

What would be the point?

Robert spat a glob of black phlegm over his shoulder, then quickly looked around, trying to ignore the sound of Mark still shouting from below. It dawned on him that sometime during his pushing, the cell phone must have dropped from between his teeth.

But it wasn't as if he could call for help anyway.

The church was steeply peaked, and he was holding on to the chimney that was three-quarters of the way to the top.

There has to be a way down! There has to be!

And then he saw it; the plywood covering that he had shoved off had skidded down the roof and was now lying on the roof of an adjacent building.

Father Callahan's quarters!

It was maybe twenty feet down to that roof, and he knew that as soon as he let go of the roof, he was going to slide—there was no chance of crawling down.

I have to.

There was no other way down.

A pain in his calf suddenly struck him, the one that was missing part of the muscle and was streaked with the burn marks from Leland.

The book! his mind screamed. *You're forgetting the book!*

Robert took a deep breath, gritted his teeth, and pulled himself back up to the chimney. Mark was already halfway up.

Robert pulled out of the opening just as another shot rang out. He heard a dull *thunk* as the bullet embedded itself in the brick, but he never saw where it struck.

"Aiden! Where the fuck are you, Aiden?! He's on the roof!"

Blood coursing in his ears, Robert took another deep breath, his lungs burning from exertion and the soot, and then yanked himself up once more. In one fluid motion, he reached down into the condemned chimney and grabbed the book with one hand. Desperate to get out of there before Mark fired off another round, Robert pushed himself backward and out of the shaft.

In his zeal, he pushed too hard, and when he tried to grab the lip of the chimney again, his fingers only grazed the rough edge where the cap had once been attached.

Robert cried out, and tried desperately to grab on to anything, but it was no use.

Before he knew it, Robert was sliding on his stomach, careening down the roof of the church, book in hand.

Chapter 21

ROBERT SCREAMED AS HE tried to grab on to the worn shingles with his one free hand. His body skipped over top a raised nail, and it scraped deep into his abdomen. At the last second, he managed to turn onto his side before it caught beneath his sternum. Blood seeped from the wound and started to soak either side of his now torn t-shirt.

Robert continued with his roll until he found himself on his back, but he immediately regretted his decision.

Now he could see where he was falling. And, more importantly, how far he had to go.

"Oh shit, oh shit, oh shit," he repeated over and over again. He put his hands out to either side in attempt to slow his descent, but only served to scrape the leather book cover and render his right palm raw.

His only saving grace was that the roof, like the rest of the church, was in a terrible state of disrepair, the wound on his stomach notwithstanding; had it been newly refinished, there would've been no telling what sort of speed he might have hit.

"Oh shhhhhhhhhhhittttttttt," he shouted as he neared the end of the roof. His heels jammed on a makeshift eaves-trough and, unable to stop himself, he was catapulted forward. His arms pinwheeled as he flew through the air, and the wind tore the book from his hand. It was almost comical the way his arms flailed as he tried desperately to grab the book, while at the same time trying to brace himself for the landing.

It was only about a four-foot drop to the top of the Father Callahan's adjacent quarters, and when Robert landed on the heel of his right hand and his left knee, his momentum was such that his neck whipped forward. His chin smacked against the flat roof, and stars flashed across his vision.

Fighting the darkness that threatened to encompass him, Robert spat a glob of blood and tried to force himself to his feet. His right wrist immediately gave way, and only at the last second was he able to prevent himself from smashing his face again.

Somehow, Robert managed to make his way to his feet, only to end up on all fours again when his left leg gave out. Gritting his teeth against the pain, he started to half crawl, half scamper forward. Then he saw the book lying open, face down, by the edge of the second roof, and he got what was either a third or fourth wind. He found that if he leaned heavily on his right leg, and dragged his left, he could limp forward at a decent clip. During his horrible descent, he hadn't forgotten that there were two men, two armed men, two *soldiers*, out to kill him.

Without pausing, Robert scooped up the book with his good hand, and then continued to the edge of roof.

It was another seven or eight feet down, but there was some fairly lush looking shrubbery beneath that he hoped would break his fall. He debated looking for another way down, a ladder, maybe, but the sound of another gunshot somewhere behind him rendered a more calculated way down a non-option.

He jumped.

Or, more aptly, he flung his body awkwardly over the edge of the roof. Although this fall was considerably shorter than his previous one, it ended the same way—in pain.

The shrubbery did little to break his fall, but he had somehow managed to land mostly on his good ankle. This time, Robert tried to roll forward like some sort of injured, amateur free runner, and he actually did a decent job of lessening the brunt of the impact.

Still, the book went flying and he felt more pain shoot up his legs. Only adrenaline drove him forward. Through blurred, teary vision, after somehow making it back to his feet, he caught sight of his car just across the street.

It can't be, he thought as he slowly shambled toward the Chevy. *It can't be.*

After all of the horrible luck that had plagued him over the past year or so, Robert didn't think it possible that he could actually escape from two trained assassins. Bending only to scoop up the book, Robert continued trudging forward.

...forty yards...thirty...twenty...

He heard the crack of a gunshot, but he didn't slow.

...ten...five...

And then, miraculously, Robert was at the car, and he yanked the driver's side door open. He didn't so much enter his rented vehicle as collapse into it.

Breathing rapidly, he tossed the book on the passenger seat before reaching for the keys in his pocket. He was tempted to pause for a moment, to succumb to the false comfort of the vehicle, to perhaps assess the extent of his many injuries.

But nothing had changed. Aiden and Mark were still out there. Still, he was helpless to prevent his wandering eyes to at least glance at the mess on his stomach. His shirt had been torn nearly to the collar, and a thick, deep cut ran from his belly button to just below his chest. Blood was smeared across his skin.

He threw his head back against the headrest, and his ear flared with pain from where the bullet had grazed him.

Sobbing now, Robert snaked the keys out of his pocket and jammed them in the ignition. He fired the car into drive, but before he could press the gas pedal, something cold and hard pressed into the groove where his neck met the back of his skull.

"I want you to drive real slow, Robert," Aiden said calmly from the backseat. "Real slow."

Chapter 22

"WHY ARE YOU DOING this? What do you want?"

Dozens of other questions rifled through Robert's brain, but he figured it best to start with the most obvious. When there was no answer, he glanced up to the rearview mirror, and realized that Aiden wasn't even looking at him anymore—he was staring blankly out the window. Thankfully, he had lowered the gun—it was presumably now aimed at his spine through the seat—but Robert wasn't foolhardy enough to think that he was out of danger.

But he *had* been a fool when he had thought that he could actually outsmart, outrun, and generally outperform Aiden and Mark. In fact, he wouldn't have been surprised if Mark shouting into the secret room hadn't been a ploy all along to get him to bring the book to Aiden waiting in his car.

Did they see my car when they arrived? Is that why they never left? When they spoke about finding the book, were they really speaking about finding me?

Aiden wasn't providing him any answers, despite his pestering questions. The only thing that the man with the stubble in the backseat did was tell him turn every few minutes. Other than that, he was either lost in thought or, more likely, simply ignoring him.

Now, as Robert's eyes again darted up into the rearview, he saw the man take a circular tin out of his pocket. He packed a wad of chewing tobacco into his bottom lip, then he reached forward and grabbed Robert's empty coffee cup from the holder between the front seats.

He removed the lid and spat into it.

"Turn left here," he instructed, his eyes going to the window again. Robert's eyes returned to the road.

He was in a random subdivision in a small town near El-loree, South Carolina, one of many that he had driven through over the last hour that all looked the same. In fact, he had driven through so many of these dinky streets that he might have convinced himself that the street that Aiden told him to turn on this time—Harmond Avenue—sounded familiar.

"Where are we going?" he asked again.

No response.

As their meandering drive eked past the hour mark, Robert's adrenaline had all but fled him. And in its place came pain.

His ankle was throbbing, and his stomach and chest burned from where the nail had cut him. The coppery taste of blood from where he had bit his tongue lingered like halitosis, and his chin ached. Ironically, the least painful was the bullet that had grazed his ear.

His back hurt too, and there was something sharp digging into the spot just above his hip.

They drove for several more minutes before Robert started to panic. Either that, or he had worked up his nerve; given his present state, it could have been either.

"Why are you doing this, Aiden? I mean, I helped you guys at Seaforth…what have I done wrong? What does Sean want with me?"

At the mention of Seaforth, Aiden's eyes flicked up and he spat into the cup. For a moment, Robert thought that the man was finally going to answer, but then he pressed his lips together obstinately.

"Left here," he ordered. It was unnerving that the man wasn't even looking when he gave directions. It was as if he was just choosing at random.

Robert had had it. Instead of turning, he jammed the car into park and whipped his head around. Aiden didn't react the way he had hoped, but at least he had the man's attention now.

"Look, I don't know what you want with me" —he reached over and grabbed the book from the passenger seat and tossed it into the back—"but if you want the book? Take it. You want to kill me? Do it. At least then I'll be with Amy." His voice hitched. "Let me ask you something: what would you do? Do you have a family? Kids?" Predictably, there was no response. Robert, did, however, perceive a slight change in the man's expression. It softened ever so slightly. "Well, I have a daughter. And she's trapped on the other side—I thought that this book could help me understand better why she's there, why she couldn't fucking just die like a normal person. And more importantly, I thought it could tell me how I can get her *back*. That's it—that's all I want. I don't want any of Sean's money, I don't want to partake in any more of his suicide missions. I just want Amy back. I don't care about my brother, my father, my fucking friends. Nothing. Just Amy."

Robert gritted his teeth and stared. He couldn't believe that he had risked his life for this stupid book, and now he had basically handed it to Sean. But what else could he do?

Even his candidness surprised him. But he was sick of these games, of skirting the truth. He was too tired, sore, and weak to lie, either to himself or to others.

Aiden spat again.

"You done?" He pulled the gun back into view. "Drive."

Robert shook his head.

"No, no fucking way. You can shoot me for all I care, but I'm not going to drive anymore. I'm fucking done driving."

Aiden squinted as he sized him up, and Robert held his ground. Eventually, the man sighed, and used the muzzle of the gun to scratch at the stubble on his cheek.

"If we wanted you dead, you wouldn't be around anymore, you know that, right?"

Now it was Robert's turn to remain silent.

"Look, you're right. Sean wants the book, and now I have it. But we don't want you dead...if you were dead, there would be bigger problems, bigger fish that wouldn't be happy. I don't really know why they are going to all this trouble for one little book, or what it means, or anything about your daughter. I just know that I was told to find the book, and I figured the best way to do that was to find you." He looked over at the book that was lying on the seat beside him. "And it worked."

"Why do you want the book?"

Aiden shook his head.

"I don't. Sean and the others do."

"Who are these others?"

"Robert, you want some advice?"

Robert threw up his arms.

"No, I don't want advice. What I want is answers, and evidently you either don't know, or are unwilling to give them to me."

Aiden spat again, then moved the wad of chew to the other side with his tongue.

"A year ago, I was a regular guy—a family guy, a fucking accountant. Then my life gets flipped upside down, and everything I loved was lost. And that's just the beginning. Next, I find out that everything I believed in was wrong, a fucking lie—even my past was a lie. A fucking absolute *lie*."

"I know how it feels, Robert," the man said, for once showing a scintilla of emotion.

"How? How is that possible?" Robert nearly shouted.

The man closed up again.

"My advice, take it or leave it, is just to put all this behind you and move on. Go find a new life for yourself, Robert. It's not too late. Believe me. Start a new life."

Robert just glared at Aiden. Even though he was clearly trying to be helpful, compassionate, his words rang hollow.

He couldn't possibly have any insight into what Robert was going through.

"Now are you going to drive?"

Robert shook his head, and Aiden raised the gun.

"Then you are going to get out and walk." His eyes hardened. "And if you don't, I'll drag you out of the goddamn car."

Chapter 23

ROBERT WATCHED IN SHEER wonderment as the car that he had driven to South Carolina pealed off without him, with Aiden in the driver seat.

What the fuck just happened?

For a long while, he just watched the dust swirl about, mesmerized by the random patterns and shapes that appeared, then just as quickly faded away. His eyes burned; his wrist, chest, and leg hurt.

His head throbbed, and fatigue threatened to take him then.

A woman walking a dog suddenly turned the corner, but when she caught a glimpse of him, she abruptly changed course and crossed to the other side of the street. She had to basically drag the snarling poodle with her. When she pulled a cell phone from her purse and continued to stare at him over her shoulder as she sped away, Robert snapped out of his stupor.

Covered in soot, ear bleeding, shirt torn, he must have looked like someone who had just escaped from Chernobyl.

I have to get out of here.

Robert limped away from the woman, electing to head the way that she had come. Sometime during his adventures in the chimney and on the church roof, he had lost his cell phone. And without it, he was at a loss for which direction he should head. To orient himself, he opted to head back in the direction of Callahan's church, but that too proved impossible. Aiden had instructed him to make so many left and right turns, sometimes two or three of the same in a row, that he had no idea how to get back.

And perhaps that had been by design.

If I wanted you dead, you wouldn't be here. Besides, others would be upset.

Robert shook his head and tried to focus.

Going to the police wasn't an option, either, as no explanation he could come up with would keep him out of the loony bin. Remembering the way the woman had quickly grabbed her phone, he was of the mind that if he stayed out in the open any longer, he was going to be speaking to the police whether he wanted to or not.

So Robert did what he had done in the church and at Seaforth: he let his mind go and followed the patterns of dust in the air.

After nearly a half hour of wandering in what seemed like circles, he arrived very near where he started, where the spooked woman on the phone had noticed him.

Robert stopped and closed his eyes, fighting back tears of frustration.

Stop with the self-pity…Amy is out there. You need to keep going.

His eyes snapped open, and he realized that he had turned around and was now staring at a house, a modest colonial, with an American flag hanging from the porch.

"What the hell?" he whispered.

Robert recognized the house; not the style or the build or the color scheme, but this *exact* house.

And it was a place that he knew well.

It was his grandfather's house.

Floored, Robert closed his eyes again, thinking that maybe it was just a mirage brought on by the pain and exhaustion.

But it *was* still there when he opened them again.

The last time he had been to the house had been following the death of his parents, Alex and Helen Watts, more than ten years prior. He had since lost touch with his grandpa, for no other reason than he had been too engrossed in his own life.

But…how? What are the odds?

Of course, Grandpa lived in Santee, South Carolina, which was near Elloree, but...

His eyes moved to the neighboring houses.

...but the "subdivision" was composed of only one or two houses back then. Now they were squished together like sardines in a tin.

Robert recalled how Aiden had seemed to be randomly choosing streets to turn on, and thought that maybe his decisions hadn't been so random after all.

Did he take pity on me? Dropped me near somewhere I was familiar with?

He couldn't see how Aiden would have known about where his grandfather lived, but Sean might. Sean seemed to know a lot more than he was letting on.

Robert swallowed hard and took a step forward, then another, testing the ground each time to make sure that it was solid.

The large front steps were difficult to navigate in his present state, and Robert felt himself getting dizzy with every passing moment. He reached out and grabbed the banister, squeezing it tightly, trying to fight the vertigo that suddenly threatened to overwhelm him.

It was a losing battle.

His eyelids fluttered, and when he went to take another step forward, his vision went double and he somehow landed on the outside of his foot.

Robert lost consciousness even before his body collapsed against the screen door.

***

There was a girl standing on the beach, her head down, her hair hanging in front of her face. Robert wanted to run to her, to wrap her up tightly in his arms, but he found himself unable to move.

He didn't need to look down to know that the black, tarry hands were holding him in place. Another figure appeared behind the girl, just a blurry shadow at first. Eventually, however, the figure became more solid, and his heart sunk in his chest.

He recognized the black hat, the faded jean jacket.

"Amy?" he whispered. "Amy, what are you doing here? Why haven't you...why haven't you joined the Sea?"

The girl didn't answer. Instead, she just shrugged.

"Is it—is it because of *him?*"

Leland started to raise his head, and Robert picked up the unpleasant, grating sound of laughter.

The man's head moved impossibly slowly, tilting backward so that the shadow that covered his face slowly started to peel back like a nylon mask. A smiling mouth came into view, one that was filled with hundreds of tiny, pointed teeth. Robert redoubled his efforts to run, only this time he wanted to run away, rather than toward the duo.

It was a cowardly move. He should have been expending all of his effort trying to rescue Amy, not run away from her, but he couldn't help himself.

Because he knew who the demon really was, and he didn't want to see.

The man tilted his head all the way back now, the laughter becoming more bestial as his throat was extended.

And then the mask slipped away completely, and Robert found himself staring into his own reflection.

Chapter 24

WHEN ROBERT OPENED HIS eyes, his throat was raw from screaming. Someone suddenly appeared at his side, holding his shoulders, saying something unintelligible, and Robert flailed furiously at his hands.

"Stay away! Don't touch me! It's not me! *It's not me!*"

"Robert!" the man said sternly.

"Stay away!"

But the man's grip was strong, and Robert was spent. They clamped down hard on his shoulders, locking him in place, and he gave up his struggle. Blinking rapidly, he finally managed to clear the tears from his eyes.

An old man stared down at him with soft green eyes surrounded by a network of creases. His mouth, equally lined, was pressed into a thin line.

"Grandpa?" Robert asked softly. He didn't quite believe what he was seeing, but he just went with it. After all, this was one of the least strange things that had happened to him recently.

"Robert, what the hell are you doing here? And what happened to you? Jesus Christ, you look like you were trapped in a coal mine? And the screams…"

Robert tried to sit up, but winced at the pain that coursed through his entire body.

"It's a long story…"

"I've got time."

Robert sighed.

How long has it been since we've seen each other? Ten years?

A pang of guilt struck him then; he hadn't even thought to invite him to Wendy or Amy's funeral.

His own granddaughter…

"Help me up, Grandpa."

The man put his hands on his back and gently helped him into a seated position. Robert winced, but once he was sitting up, he felt better. A quick glance down revealed that the scratch on his chest had been covered with a series of thick bandages that covered its length.

Noticing his gaze, the old man offered, "Tried my best, but it was your grandma that was the nursing one, not I. But I guess you knew that."

Robert touched the bandage gingerly, the unsightly bruising on his wrist making him nauseated again.

It was real—it was as real as the bandage on his ear.

"Here," the man said, holding out two pills in one hand, and a glass of water in the other, "take these. Then you better let me know what's going on."

Robert's throat was still raw from inhaling all of the soot in the converted chimney, and it took him three tries before he was able to force the pills down.

Eventually he finished the water, then looked up at his grandfather.

"Marv, you have anything stronger?"

The man smiled a sad smile.

"I thought you might ask."

With a groan of his own, Marvin Watts rose from his kneeling position and left the room. A minute later, he returned with two empty glasses and a bottle of scotch. He poured three fingers into each, and then retrieved a cigar from the humidor on the table and held it up.

"Mind if I smoke?"

The last thing Robert felt like was inhaling any more smoke, but he nodded anyway. After all, it was the man's house, and he was only a guest.

"Go ahead," he said, reaching for the scotch with his good hand. It was no 25-year Glenlivet, but that didn't matter. It warmed his stomach, and numbed his mouth and throat.

That was what mattered.

Marvin set about cutting and then lighting his cigar, and as he swished away the initial cloud of smoke from his head, he spoke.

"Before you start, I owe you an apology, Robert. I heard — shit — I heard about Wendy and Amy and I didn't even send a card. I ain't got no excuses, but it's been tough, you know? Out here all alone. A man can forget his graces, his manners. I'm very sorry for your loss."

Robert blinked.

He's sorry? I never even brought Amy out here to meet him.

The one time that he had suggested they drive down south, Wendy had struck him down.

'Drive? In that heat? When's the last time you even spoke to him? Are you sure he's even still alive?'

Robert stared at the man puffing on his cigar across from him.

He was real.

Probably.

"Marv, it's my fault, I should have —"

The man waved his hand in a way that only he could, marking the end of the discussion.

"Throughout a man's life, he is forced to make decisions for his family," he said, as if reading Robert's mind. "Ones that maybe he ain't none too proud of. I get that. Now tell me what in the Lord's name you are doing here."

Robert stared at the brown liquid in the bottom of his glass. He felt conflicted; he couldn't rightly tell Marvin the real reason why he was here, as doing so would invariably put him in danger. Instead, he decided to skirt the question and ask his own.

"Marv, can you tell me about Mom and Dad?"

There was a pause, inciting Robert to look up. Marvin was staring at the end of his cigar as he rolled it between thumb and forefinger.

"You know, when I dragged you inside, for some reason I just knew that this was what it was about. It don't make sense, I know, but I just got this feeling. And this whole time you were passed out—three hours—I was gettin' ready to answer the question." He finally met Robert's gaze and shrugged. "They was going to tell you, Robert—eventually. But you know as good as any how life is. Shit happens, comes up, messes with timelines, with your head. I think, deep down, Alex wanted to find your brother first, and when he couldn't do that, he was too guilty to tell you. Helen sat right there, right where you are now, bawling her eyes out, trying to convince Alex to tell you. I mean, shit, you were all growed up then. But they died before they got a chance, I guess. Shit happens. What was I supposed to do? Tell you at the funeral? What would be the point to flip your life upside down?"

Robert's hands were shaking so badly that he feared he was going to spill scotch all over the carpeting.

"It's true," he whispered. "It's true."

He brought the scotch to his lips and took a sip, while Marv continued as if he hadn't even heard him.

"Your parents tried for a long time to get pregnant normally. A long, long time. They tried to adopt, but it was going to take at least two or three years. The most patient of folk, your parents weren't. At the time, there was some other shit—voodoo-type shit in the swamp…but, another story for another day. Anyways, they had almost given up when they met the priest."

"Father Callahan," Robert said.

Marvin made a face, then took a puff of his cigar.

"Father Callahan," he confirmed. "But the priest, he never told them about your brother. That came later, much later."

"How'd they find out about him?"

Marv shrugged.

"Your father never told me—he just said he found out."

"What else do you know, Marv? About me? About my past?"

Marvin took a long time before answering.

"Nothing. Not really. I mean, your dad tried to find out as much as he could from the priest, but the man was as tight-lipped as they come. When Alex came to him about the news of your brother, the man shut up for good. Your mother and grandmother liked to go to his Sunday service, whenever she was around—I hated it, personally, but I went along with her, you know, compromise 'n all that. But after your dad told Father Callahan about your brother, the man rarely showed up at the church anymore. Soon I stopped seeing him altogether. There were some rumors going around town at the time, but they were just rumors."

"Rumors? What kind of rumors?"

Marvin puffed on his cigar.

"Oh, you know, the typical shit they say of an aging priest. Lost his faith, lost interest in God. There was even some shit about botched exorcisms—take that for what it's worth. I had a friend that worked at the library after he retired from the service—God only knows why—and he said that the priest was in there all the time with a book, asking questions about Latin or some shit. I dunno, the guy is old—maybe he had Alzheimer's or something or that other thing...the thing that soldiers get."

"PTSD."

"Yeah, that's it. Anyways, the neighbors are saying that since of a couple months ago, there ain't been nobody at the church. Not even someone to take out the trash. Maybe he just up and left, turned Buddhist or something."

Robert finished his scotch. "He's dead, Grandpa."

Marvin took another drag of his cigar. Without looking at him, he said, "Yeah, and something tells me that that has to do with why you look the way you do."

Robert said nothing.

"Look, Robert, we might not be blood, but I've always considered you a Watts. Loved you as one, too, if in my own way. Even though we lost touch since your parents died, I'm here for you—you can tell me as little or as much as you want, and I'll stay mum about it." He took a sip of his scotch, then leveled his gaze at Robert. "Just wanted you to know that."

Robert swallowed hard. There was so much that Marvin didn't know, so much that he wanted to tell him, but the truth was, he too enjoyed his time with his grandpa. Which was exactly why he would tell him nothing.

"I...I need to get cleaned up," Robert said simply. It felt wrong, and he felt dirty for taking and giving nothing, but it was the best he could do.

Marvin leaned back in his chair, doing a poor job of hiding his displeasure. He grabbed the remote and aimed it across the room at the old-fashioned tube TV.

"You know where the shower is. Some fresh towels under the sink, and you can check my closet for something to wear."

"Thank you," Robert said. The pills had started to take effect much more quickly than he had expected, making him wonder if Marvin hadn't given him something stronger than run-of-the-mill Advil. He grunted and forced himself to his feet. "Thank you, Marv. And for what it's worth, I've missed you."

Chapter 25

ROBERT FELT TEN TIMES better after cleaning the soot and blood from his body. Putting on a clean shirt, a little too big, a little too out of style, and a pair of jeans that fit the same mold made him feel even better.

Still, when he made his way down the hallway to the front room again, his limp had become more pronounced. He had just entered the living room when Marvin spoke, not bothering to look away from the television.

"Can you believe this shit? Found a girl dead, locked in a cage in the basement of some Wall Street asshole's apartment. Her fingers had been eaten. *Eaten.* Police say he had this whole setup in his basement...like a horror movie. They say they would never have found her, but for a vent cover that slipped and the smell eventually drifted upward..."

That was the thing about Marv: he could be so enthralled by something one minute, but then he would just let it go and move on to something else with a simple snap of his fingers.

Robert, unfortunately, was not blessed with the same proclivity, and he envied the man.

"One thing I still don't understand, Marv," he started, "is why I don't remember. I mean, I was four or so when I was adopted, right?"

Marv shrugged.

"About that, yeah."

"Then why didn't I remember?"

Marv shrugged.

"I don't know. I mean, you lived with Father Callahan for a while, and you know what they say about little boys and priests."

Robert frowned. Marv was like Cal in the sense that his jokes weren't always the most appropriate in either timing or in nature. His eyes drifted from the television to the couch that Marv had somehow hoisted him onto when he had passed out. He could make out his outline in soot, complete with dark maroon bloodstains.

Robert felt bad for the old, lonely man sitting in his La-Z-Boy. He had probably been living the same existence since his wife died, and then his son. And Robert had ignored him. If things hadn't taken such an abrupt turn, he could have seen himself in the same position after Wendy and Amy's passing.

"Marv? You ever…you ever see Alex after the accident?"

The man turned around and leaned over the back of his chair and squinted at him.

"What do you mean?"

"I mean, did you see him? After the accident?"

The man paused, and Robert thought he saw something cross of his face. But then it was gone.

"No," he said, turning back to the TV. "I told you, your grandma was into that stuff, not me."

Robert stood there for a moment, thinking about the response. He wondered just how many people in this world had seen their loved ones after they died, either as they left their bodies and crossed over to the Marrow, or as lingering quiddity stuck on the wrong side.

How many of them had been called delusional, or accused of being unable to deal with their grief, and just plain crazy?

He also wondered how many of them had resorted to drugs and alcohol because of what they had seen.

"The keys are on the table. Take the car, Robert."

Robert made a face.

"What? No, I—"

The man, still facing the TV, held up his hand, silencing him.

And that was another thing about Marv. Even Alex couldn't change the man's mind once it had been set.

"They're right beside your album."

Album?

Robert's eyes darted to the table, and his breath caught in his throat when he spied the blue photo album that he had taken from the church lying atop it.

It seemed impossible that it had stayed with him this whole time, that during his fall from the roof, driving in the car, and collapsing on Marv's porch he hadn't dropped it somewhere along the way.

But evidently he hadn't.

Robert limped as fast as he could to the couch and sat, not caring about the soot that puffed up around him as he did.

Hands trembling, he grabbed the album and opened it to the first page.

It was the same black-and-white photograph as before, depicting a smiling Father Callahan and a stern-faced Sean Sommers. Robert flipped to the next page, his hands shaking so much that the jiggling photo was making him nauseated. He wasn't sure why, but he was suddenly terrified.

The next photograph was of a child of about six years, sitting on the floor of the church. Robert didn't recognize her, and quickly turned the page. The next photograph was almost identical, only the girl was younger than the first. He flipped through the next few images waiting for something to justify his rapid heartrate and the sweat on his brow. It appeared that Father Callahan had taken a picture of everyone that he had rescued or housed over the years, young or old.

Kendra, the little girl that he had played hide-and-seek with in his memories, was the seventh girl. Robert ran his finger gently over her image, hearing her voice in his head.

'Quick, in here!'

They had been friends, he was sure of it, even if she had been much different than he—outgoing, strangely mature for her age.

Where are you now, Kendra?

A tear slipped from his cheek and landed on her face. He wiped it away, then turned to the next photograph before he became overwhelmed with emotion. It wasn't so much that he longed for a friend that he barely remembered, but that he longed for just *remembering*.

The woman was older than the others, in her late-twenties, maybe, and unlike the girls, she wasn't smiling. Robert leaned in close, squinting at the photo.

It looks like...like...

He dropped the album.

It was Christine, the one that he had been hiding from that fateful day with Kendra. But it was also the woman from Carson's cell, the one that had been holding Father Callahan's hand.

Robert gasped.

She had been at the church under Father Callahan's care, she had to have been, but something terrible had happened to her—he knew this, like he'd known that the book would be in the secret room. Something had happened that had sent her on a different path, had turned her against Father Callahan, and in the process made her a useful pawn for Carson and Leland.

His brother and his father.

Robert shuddered, and quickly flipped the page. The next photograph was of two girls, twins, their matching gap-toothed smiles aimed directly at the camera.

Not recognizing them, Robert quickly flipped the page. There was a reason why Father Callahan had left this stashed away, a reason that he wanted him to see it. And it wasn't for Christine, or Kendra, or even…

Robert's train of thought froze as he found himself staring at his own image as a young boy. He had never seen a photo of himself this young. His hair was stark white, cut straight across his forehead, and he had a small, upturned nose and heavy cheeks. Unlike the girls, however, he wasn't smiling. Holding a small truck in his hand, he was on one knee in a room that he didn't recognize. His dark eyes were locked on the camera, but they also seemed to be looking *through* it.

Robert swallowed hard and inspected the image closely, trying to figure out if there was something in it that he was supposed to see. In the background, he made out a small cot with what looked like sheets balled up at the end of it, but the rest of the image was blanketed in shadows.

What? What is it that you wanted me to see, Father?

Breathing rapidly now, Robert turned to the next photograph, the final one of the album.

His face sunk, his heart dropped into his stomach. In the photo, her face was different, younger, rounder.

But it was *her*.

"No," he moaned. "It's impossible."

Chapter 26

"GOT THE BOOK," AIDEN said, his voice and demeanor as cold and deadpan as ever.

Sean looked up and couldn't help but smile. It had been at least a decade since he had given the book to Father Callahan with strict instructions not to show it to anyone. At the time, the man in the cloak had said it was necessary, that it should never be in the same place as a Guardian. Back then, Sean had just shrugged and agreed. But now...now that he knew the power of the book, he realized that he had missed it.

That he had longed for it.

Sean reached out and took the book from Aiden, his hand subconsciously caressing the rough leather cover. His fingers began to trace the letters engraved on the cover—*Inter vivos et mortuos*—and he felt his smile grow.

It was *the* book—the book that had started it all.

"Good. Did you see Robert? Was he there?"

Aiden stared at him.

"No. He wasn't there. Just the book."

Sean screwed up his face. He was beginning to think that getting the man involved in this was a mistake, just as the man in the cloak had told him. Still, he had served his purpose: he had helped him with the Harlops, at Pinedale, and at Seaforth. He had even dealt with his brother.

But Sean had underestimated the man, that much was certain. He was just an accountant, and he was never supposed to have been this involved—and Sean had told him too much.

An image of Robert in Seaforth, his hands up, demanding that the guard stop, flashed in his mind.

And then there was that, too—whatever it was.

"Any idea where he is?" he asked absently. Aiden was good, but he had a sneaking suspicion that if Robert wanted to remain lost, he would manage it.

There was just so much about the man that even Sean didn't know.

Aiden shook his head.

"No. He hasn't returned to the estate, either, as far as I can tell."

Sean, still caressing the cover, thought about that for a moment.

If he wasn't at the estate, then where was he? Part of the reason why he had given the man the house was so that he could keep his eye on him. And that was what the money was for, too. It was all about making sure that he stayed put, that if he ever needed him again, then he would be *there*.

That if any other Carson types came looking for a Guardian, that Sean would know exactly where he was.

But now he was gone, and if the pressure in Sean's chest was any indication, this wasn't over yet.

As long as Leland was still hanging around on the shores of the Marrow, this would never end. The only way to make him leave, as far as the book was concerned, was for him to absolve the self.

And Sean couldn't envision a scenario in which that actually happened.

"You want me to keep an eye on the estate? The others?"

Sean contemplated this for a moment.

"No...yes," he corrected himself.

Thoughts of Robert in Seaforth, doing that strange thing with his hands, ordering the quiddity to stand down, came to him again.

That wasn't in the book.

Maybe there are other options for Leland, and for Robert, too, Sean thought.

He shook his head, and stroked the cover of the book even more aggressively.

Maybe there is more to learn than what is in the book.

"Yes," Sean agreed, more strongly this time. "Keep an eye on Robert's friends. And if he comes back, let me know — let me know right away."

PART III – Intractable

Chapter 27

"HE'LL COME," JONAH SAID, nodding vigorously. Blood still dripped from his head, a slow, steady stream, forcing him to continually wipe it away with the back of his hand.

Shelly had brained him pretty good, Cal realized, as he stared at the four-inch cut that ran from the top of his head to just above his eyebrow. She had brained him good, but it hadn't seemed to even faze the little fucker. If anything, it only seemed to make him even more despicable.

Cal shook his head.

"No—no he won't. He left and isn't coming back," Cal said, trying not to sound dejected. He tensed his hands, and the rope holding them together bit into his wrists. He glanced over for support from Shelly, who was also tied to one of the kitchen chairs, her chin to her chest, but she remained silent.

"Oh, he'll be back, all right," Jonah contended.

Cal and Shelly were in the sitting room, both tied to a chair, with Jonah standing in front of them, the broken tripod gripped in his hand like a spear. Allan was lying face down on the floor, still unconscious. A dinner plate-sized pool of blood surrounded his mouth and nose from where Jonah had struck him. He was so completely and utterly still that the only thing convincing Cal that he was still alive was the bubbles that formed in the blood every few seconds when he exhaled.

And then there were the dead.

There were eleven of them, all told, all in various states of decay. They stood behind him and Shelly, not terribly unlike how the men in the prison had been standing—their hands limp at their sides, heads hung low, and unlike Allan on the floor, *not* breathing.

"You seem pretty fucking sure of yourself."

Jonah giggled.

"Yep, yep, yep. Robert'll come."

Cal gritted his teeth. The selfish part of him hoped that Robert *did* show up, that he put this man and the quiddity behind him in their place. But despite their recent differences, he still loved the man. He wouldn't have blamed Robert if he was gone, to have forever left this filth in the rearview.

If anyone had reason to up and be a hermit, it would've been Robert. The only thing the man had left was...well, him and Shelly. And Cal wasn't sure that they were worth whatever the man in the bloodstained Mickey Mouse t-shirt before him had in store.

"Give it up, you freak. Robert's gone, he doesn't give a shit about us. So why don't you just tell your fucking dead goons to touch us and send us on our way, how about that? Send us to see the fucking Goat, Leland, whatever the hell he is. Cause when I get there, I know exactly what choice I'm going to make."

Cal looked over at Shelly when he spoke, but she couldn't hold his gaze.

She was crying.

Jonah, on the other hand, was amused.

"Oh, I can't really tell them what to do. Only Carson can do that. But I guess...if Robert..." the man hesitated before continuing, "No, he'll be back. He'll be back."

"Wait—Carson? *Carson*?" Now it was Cal's turn to laugh. "Now you've really fucking lost it, bud. Carson's dead. I don't know how you managed to tell these fucking spirits to do your bidding, but I can assure you that it wasn't Carson who did it."

"You're wrong. Carson Ford is very much alive. In fact, he should be—" Jonah checked his watch. "—he should be here very soon."

Cal leaned as far forward in his chair as his bindings would allow and eyed up Jonah in an attempt to determine if he was, in fact, insane.

Carson was dead—Sean had told him so. Sean had told him that Robert himself had killed him—shot him dead. His own brother, which was the reason why Cal figured that Robert had left them, to try and deal with what he had done.

Carson couldn't be alive...could he?

No, Cal concluded. Jonah was just a run-of-the-mill psychopath—a demented psychopath who somehow managed to order the dead around to do his bidding.

He shook his head.

"You're wrong, Elmer Fudd. Robert ain't coming."

Jonah giggled again.

"Wanna know how I know he's coming?" he asked.

"Oh, please, do tell."

Jonah hooked a chin over to Shelly, who was now staring intently. She hadn't said anything for a long while now, and Cal hoped that she would pipe up with a biting remark, showing that she was still okay. That she was still Shelly. But she didn't; Shelly remained silent.

"Because of her."

And this time Shelly did reply, but her response lacked the vehemence that Cal expected.

"He won't come back just for me," she said softly. "He's staying away *because* of me."

"No, no, silly girl. Not *because* of you, but because of the baby in your belly."

Cal recoiled.

"Wha—Shelly, what's he talking about?"

"Nothing," she said quickly. "He doesn't know anything."

But Shelly's expression belied her words: her face drooped and her jaw went slack. And in that moment, Cal knew what Jonah said was true.

It can't be.

But it could be, and it *was*. Shelly being pregnant explained her weight gain, her wild, even for her, mood swings.

"Oh, you're pregnant all right," Jonah said. He flicked his tongue out and wagged it, spraying blood on his chin. "I can smell it on ya."

Chapter 28

ROBERT KNEW THERE WAS something wrong even before he made it to the front gate outside the Harlop Estate.

It was his chest—pressure was building just behind his breastbone, making it difficult for him to take a full breath. It was a sensation he had felt before, and he was becoming oddly comfortable with the implications: there were quiddity here, which meant that Shelly and Cal and Allan were in danger.

He pulled the door to Marv's Tempo open even before it was fully stopped. Then he squeezed through the opening in the gate, thankful that he didn't have to engage the squeaky motorized mechanism. As he neared the front of the house, he stooped low, a difficult act given his aching body, and stuck to the shadows by the edge of the fountain.

The light in the front room was on, and as he neared the sitting room window, he caught sight of a man tied to a chair.

"No," he whispered as he continued to move. It was Cal, and the man's face was sunken.

Then he saw the dead hovering behind him, and Robert froze.

***

"He won't come back, because he doesn't even know!" Shelly shouted, suddenly recanting her objections to the fact that she was pregnant. "You fucking psycho! It doesn't matter what you do to us, *because Robert is not coming back!* Tell Carson he's going to need to find someone else to participate in his sick game—to open the rift in the Marrow."

Cal didn't like the way Jonah was staring down his long nose at Shelly, all the demented humor suddenly gone from his face. As he watched, the man put his tongue back into his mouth.

"Don't call me a psycho," he said quietly. Cal watched as Jonah tightened his grip on the broken camera tripod leg.

"Fuck you, you fucking *psycho!*"

The man took a step toward Shelly, holding the tripod out in front of him like a lance.

"Don't," he ordered.

"Psycho," Shelly spat back.

Jonah moved quickly for such a big man, closing the distance between them in a fraction of a second. Then he brought the sharp end of the broken tripod legs down in a sweeping arc.

"No!" Cal shouted, but even flexing as hard as he could against the ropes, there was nothing he could do.

Shelly screamed, and Cal expected to see a geyser of blood. To his relief, it appeared as if the man had missed his mark.

"Please," he begged, "don't—"

But then Jonah moved to one side and Cal realized that the man hadn't missed; he had found his mark. Only he had more sinister intentions than just gutting her.

The front of Shelly's blouse had been sliced open, revealing her full breasts behind a lacy black bra.

"No!" Cal shouted, but was helpless to watch as Jonah lunged at her bare skin, his full weight nearly toppling the chair.

He sucked and kissed at her breasts like a wild animal. When he tore her bra off, revealing her small, dark nipples, Cal looked away, tears streaming down his face.

"Get the fuck off of her!" he yelled. He pulled so hard against the ropes that bound his hands that he felt blood start to drip into his palms.

It was no use; whatever kind of fucked up Jonah was, whatever midget brain that he had in his bald head, he had experience tying people up.

Shelly screamed again, which was quickly followed by more of the man's disgusting wet, lapping sounds.

"Get off her!" Cal shouted again. His ankles were also tied, but he was still able to flex his feet. He drove his toes into the floor, causing the chair to rise up a few inches, before coming down hard again. He repeated this motion, desperately trying to smash the chair's old wooden legs. On the third or fourth try, he heard a crack, but the wood held. When he tried to propel himself upward again, harder this time, ignoring the pain in his bound limbs, one of the quiddity suddenly stepped in front of him.

The ghost was hideous—half of her face was missing. To his horror, Cal realized that he could see directly into her head through her face. His guts roiled as he expected to see a brain, pulsating maybe, or a bloody wound therein, but instead it appeared as if her head had been hollowed out, like an eggshell. When she looked at him, he saw the ragged end of the optic nerve leading from the eye on that side of her head flap like tinsel in the wind.

Cal could stand the sight no longer, and he turned his face away, tasting vomit rise in his throat. But before he allowed himself the sweet release, the front door to the estate suddenly flew open, drawing his gaze up again.

"Get the fuck off her," Robert demanded as he rushed into the room.

Chapter 29

THE HIDEOUS TROLL WITH the bloody forehead leapt off Shelly and tried to turn, but at some point he had dropped his trousers and they caught around his knees.

He fell flat on his face.

As he scrambled to his feet, Cal was shocked to see that the man was smiling.

"See? I told you he would *come*. It's just too bad that I didn't get my chance to do the same." He looked at Shelly, who was bare-chested and sobbing. "But I will soon, don't you worry, sweetie."

Robert rushed toward the man, fists balled at his sides. Jonah had something in his hand, something that reflected in the lights, but Robert was so blinded by fury that he didn't appear to notice.

In fact, Cal doubted that his friend was thinking at all.

"Robbo!" he shouted, but Robert didn't stop. There was no doubt in his mind that Robert would have kept running at Jonah, and likely would have found himself in a pool of blood on the floor in a matter of seconds. But before he could reach Jonah, the window behind the fat man shattered inward.

Robert dug his heels in and came to an abrupt halt as something passed directly through Mickey Mouse's left ear before smashing into the brick fireplace on the other side of the room, sending shrapnel flying. Jonah blubbered something incoherent, then looked down at his chest in horror.

There was a watermelon-sized hole directly through the center of his belly—Cal could see Shelly's terrifying expression right through Jonah. A silence that lasted nearly three full seconds came over the room, then as if time itself had restarted, blood spilled from Jonah's mouth. His organs slipped down to fill the hole in his gut, before sliding out of him. A moment later, Jonah collapsed with a wet groan in a heap on the floor beside Allan.

"Robbo!" Cal shouted, and Robert finally turned to look at him.

The eleven dead had started to close in on him—he could smell their rotting flesh as they neared.

Startled, it took Robert a second before he acted. Cal leaned away from the woman with half a face as she reached for his chest and arm.

"Stop!" Robert shouted at the top of his lungs, while at the same time raising his hands as he had done in Seaforth. His shout drew their attention and all eleven pairs of black, coal-filled eyes turned toward Robert.

Cal watched as Robert appeared to bear down, his chest becoming concave, the crown of his head aimed toward the dead. His eyes were closed, his breathing rhythmic.

"Stop!" Robert ordered again, this time his words but a mere hiss through gritted teeth.

The dead fingers stopped moving mere inches from Cal. And yet, unlike in the prison, where the guard had been completely still, the fingers still twitched. Cal wasn't sure what that meant, but was absolutely certain that he didn't want to find out.

"Allan!" he shouted. "Allan, get the fuck up and untie me!"

The boy stirred.

"Allan! Get *up!*"

The woman in front of him snarled, and Cal felt his heart thump a mile a minute in his chest. A quick glance at Robert, and he knew that his friend wouldn't be able to hold them indefinitely. His face was turning a deep crimson and his face was slick with sweat.

"Allan!"

The boy's eyes flicked open, and for a few seconds he just blinked in the pool of blood, clearly not understanding what was happening.

"Allan!" he shouted again, trying to get his attention. "Allan!" This time Shelly joined in, and it seemed to shock the boy into full consciousness.

He rose to his feet, staggered, and then wiped the blood from his face with the back of his hand as he righted himself.

"Untie us!"

Cal was trying to keep the boy's attention, but when he looked down at Jonah, who was lying in a pile of his own bloated intestines, he knew that he had lost him. Allan doubled over and vomited on the floor.

"Allan," Robert hissed. "Please hurry—I can't hold them much longer."

Allan stood up straight, and started to whisper 'oh god,' over and over again, but finally understanding the magnitude of the situation, he started moving. Taking a wide berth around the frozen spirits, he went to Shelly first. The boy, doing his best to avoid looking at her exposed breasts, went to the ropes on her wrists. A couple of sharp tugs from behind and Shelly's hands were free. Shelly leaned forward and grabbed the bra from the floor and put it back on before tending to the ropes around her ankles.

"Help Cal!" she instructed Allan.

As Allan, so pale that he was nearly translucent, headed his way, something flashed in his periphery.

A bare-chested man covered in tattoos rushed toward Robert from the kitchen.

"Robert!" he screamed as loud as he could manage.

Chapter 30

AIDEN FLUSHED THE SPENT round from the rifle, and immediately set about replacing it. He was lying on his stomach on the grassy incline near the rear of the Harlop property, using the shadow of a large boulder to further disguise him.

There was another man inside the home; he had seen him upstairs rooting around, but after Robert had burst through the front door, Aiden hadn't been able to track him.

The other one, the fat one in the Mickey Mouse t-shirt, was dead—shot through the stomach. A clean kill, nearly instant death. Aiden had wanted a head shot, but the man was so short that he was worried about dinging Shelly if he tried to shoot over top of her. The man's gut, however, hung out to the side, making it a safer shot.

Aiden lay down again after the new round was in place, and peered through the rifle scope. He saw Robert in the center of the room, hands outstretched, his face pinched in either pain or concentration. He couldn't see the kid or Cal through the window, but Shelly was there. He smirked when she walked up and kicked the dead man in the head, sending blood flying.

She was a tough one, that Shelly. He had seen her in action at Seaforth, and he was duly impressed.

The man with the tattoos suddenly appeared, sprinting at the unsuspecting Robert from behind. Aiden exhaled, and applied pressure to the trigger, waiting for the scope to focus on the man's torso. A split second before firing, Aiden dropped the gun and rolled onto his left side.

The rock landed in the grass with a dull thud, embedding itself at least four inches in the dirt. Aiden sprang to his feet, while at the same time slipping his knife from the holster on his thigh.

"You're dead," he said simply, but the man with the Cheshire grin standing just three feet away laughed.

"Nope," Carson said, his hands squeezing the fist-sized rocks held in each hand. "Alive and well. Can't say the same for you, though."

Aiden squinted at the thin man before him. He couldn't tell if Carson was living or dead, but he wasn't about to take any chances. He held the knife out in front of him, making sure that the other man got a good look at it.

"I don't know how you got away from Seaforth, but I'm going to make sure you stay dead this time."

Carson laughed.

"So Robert's making friends everywhere he goes now, is that it? Got his boyfriends protecting him?"

"Drop the rocks," Aiden instructed, his voice monotone. "Now."

To his surprise, Carson's thin fingers unfurled and both stones fell to the ground with successive thumps.

Aiden switched his grip on the knife.

"Good, now—"

But a blinding pain in his side stole the words from his throat. He cried out and spun around, slashing at air. Pain flared on his other side, just above his hip, and he whipped around that way, catching sight of a swirl of long, dark hair.

The next attack severed his Achilles, and Aiden dropped to one knee.

He kept swinging his blade, but he would miss the woman by mere inches.

How is she this fast?

Gasping, bleeding, the blade plunged into his back, puncturing his lung from behind. This time, however, instead of being removed and readied to stick him again, this time the blade remained embedded in his body.

"Please," he croaked before his mouth filled with foam mixed with blood.

Then the blade was twisted and it nicked his heart. Aiden fell on his stomach. His eyes fluttering, he looked up to see that a woman had joined Carson at his side, his arm locked around her waist.

Carson gently guided her away, then came right up to Aiden, squatting on his haunches. Somewhere far away, he felt his head being pulled back, and then Carson was directly in his face, his breath sour with adrenaline.

"When you see my dad, tell him we're going to get him out of there soon, okay?"

And then Aiden closed his eyes for the final time.

Chapter 31

THE MAN STRUCK ROBERT in his side, sending them both careening to the ground.

"Shel! The cameras!" he heard Cal yell. The tackle forced him to release the quiddity, and with it went the pain in his chest. Feeling rushed back to his hands and fingers, but that wasn't necessarily a good thing.

Pain came with it.

But Robert wouldn't let himself be overwhelmed, not when his friends were in trouble.

He rolled onto his back, trying to catch his bearings, but before he could even suck in a fresh breath, the man was on him again. The man was in full mount, and started raining down punches. Robert got his hands up to deflect the first few blows, but eventually his hands were knocked aside. The man's knuckles cracked off his cheekbone, sending stars across his vision. Robert tried to buck him off him by thrusting his hips, but this only seemed to increase the ferocity of the blows.

A fist collided with his forehead and the back of Robert's head banged off the floor. Darkness threatened to close in, but somehow he managed one last-ditch effort to turn his head.

What the hell?

Shelly and Cal and Allan were standing across from one another, forming a sort of triangle, their cameras all pointed at the quiddity, who—

The man on top of him took a deep breath and then leaned in close.

"I'm going to enjoy eating you," he whispered.

—were still locked in place.

How? How is this possible?

The man grabbed his injured wrist and Robert screamed. He tried to struggle some more, but he was winded and exhausted. The man put his index finger into his mouth and bit down *hard*.

There was an audible crunch, and Robert shrieked.

"Allan! No!" he heard Cal shout.

Robert's eyes rolled back in his head, but not before he saw Allan stride over to him. The tattooed freak was so engrossed in chewing off his finger that he never even saw the boy coming. And he definitely didn't see the foot that collided with the side of his head, sending him sprawling.

"Allan!" It was Shelly's voice this time.

Robert, dazed, tried to focus on the sound of her voice, to use it as an anchor to fend off the threat of unconsciousness. When he managed to open his eyes again, he was too late. Whatever was holding the quiddity in place broke from the one nearest Allan, a woman who was missing half of her face. She reached out and grabbed Allan by the shoulders. Her mouth, previously slack-jawed, had become a snarl.

"No!" Robert gasped. Somewhere far away, he heard Cal and Shelly screaming, too. He blinked hard and tried to right himself as Allan and the quiddity started to fade.

Somehow Robert managed to rotate toward Allan and hold a hand up, barely noticing that the index finger was now two inches shorter than it had been when he had arrived at the Harlop Estate.

"No!" he shouted, louder this time. He bore down, and something broke in his chest.

But despite his efforts, Allan's eyes turned a pitch black and he continued to fade, all the while the dead woman started to become more solid.

No, he thought, *not her. Bring Allan back!*

But the harder he tried, the more real the dead woman became and the more ethereal Allan appeared.

"Robert! Do something!" Shelly shouted.

Robert lacked the energy to reply, to yell back 'I am! I'm fucking trying!' and instead focused all of his remaining strength.

It was no use; Allan was gone.

Robert let go then, feeling a great void inside.

The dead woman collapsed in a heap, but as he stared, she slowly raised her half-face and looked at him.

Her eyes weren't black anymore, they were green. A vibrant, penetrating green that the dead shouldn't have possessed.

She was *alive*.

The man with the tattoos had recovered from the kick to his temple and was about to pounce on Robert again, when a familiar voice spoke from near the front door.

"That's enough, Michael. *That's enough!*"

Chapter 32

"I NEVER THOUGHT I would see you again so soon, Robert." Carson shrugged. "But, Daddy wants to come out, you know? He wants to spread the word—time's a-wasting."

Robert couldn't focus. Even after releasing the quiddity, and draining the dead woman with half a face, the pressure inside him had come back. Only now it wasn't in his chest, but in his head. It was like he was buried under miles of water and all of his movements were labored, as if life was happening in slow motion.

It could have been from the blows to the face, but he didn't think so. He had been through a lot today, and nothing had felt like this.

"Neat trick with the girl, by the way. You gotta teach me how you did that."

Robert blinked, and time seemed to slow even more. He heard Shelly say something, but he couldn't make out the words.

His head was just so damn *tight*.

"No, no, no, I wouldn't do that if I were you, Shelly. Stay put. You may be tough, but you aren't a match for Bella. Besides, I would probably think twice about lowering your camera, wouldn't you? 'Less I sick the big bad quiddity on ya. How 'bout it?"

Carson paused, and Robert tried to clear his head by stretching his jaw. It didn't help.

"Robert? You still with me? I'm sorry for Michael here, sometimes he just—*ooooo*—sometimes he just gets so excited. He didn't mean it, I'm sure. Go on, tell him, Michael, tell him."

Someone grumbled.

"And you, Shelly, sorry about Jonah. He too can, well, get *excited*. But we're all friends here, aren't we? And I think it's about time that we finish with the pleasantries and get started."

Robert tried to roll onto his side, but he couldn't move.

"Robert? Robert? Time to get up, sweetheart. We have work to do. Daddy's coming home."

But instead of replying, Robert closed his eyes. He closed his eyes and started to breathe deeply.

Almost immediately, darkness pervaded his every sense; a deep, foreboding blackness that had an almost velvety texture to it. Only this time, instead of fighting it, instead of resisting the urge to fall in the Marrow, he embraced it.

But there were no specks of white, no frothing ocean, no Leland Black.

And no Amy.

Far away, he felt his heart sink into the pit that was his stomach. If nothing else, this foray to the Marrow as an observer would have allowed him to see Amy. After all, she was the only thing that was still real to him. Everything else had been taken away: his memories, his wife, his family, his life.

Only she was real. And he had to devise a way to get her back.

Words reverberated in the darkness; muffled voices—a woman's voice he had never heard before.

"Please," she pleaded, her voice gaining clarity with each word. "Please, don't hit me again. I did nothing wrong!"

The layers of darkness started to peel back, and before he knew it, Robert was staring at a dark-haired man with close-set eyes and a bulbous nose. There was sweat on his forehead, and sauce staining the corners of his lips.

And he was some kind of angry.

"Please, it wasn't my fault…it wasn't my fault, Paul."

It was the woman's voice, but for some reason it felt to Robert that the words were coming out of *his* mouth. Robert tried to look down, to catch his bearings, but he was only an observer in this strange world.

And his view was limited to what the woman saw.

The man snarled and stepped forward, his fists knotting into boulders. The woman looked down at these hairy knuckles and Robert felt his heart flutter.

"Paul?" she wept. "Please, Paul. Please—I did nothing wrong."

The man rushed at her. Hands, small hands, woman hands, went up in self-defense, but the man named Paul swatted them away with ease. And then he was upon her, punching her first in the stomach and then in the neck.

Robert felt as if he was the one being assaulted, and the air was forced out of his lungs as his diaphragm was paralyzed. When the man's knuckles hit his throat, he gasped.

The woman's hands came up again, and this time, her nails were out. She scratched at his flesh, tearing thick, shoelace-sized pieces of skin.

Robert felt her anxiety, her fear, as if his own. His or her heart—he was no longer able to distinguish between the two—was racing.

"You dare scratch me, Helen? You fucking dare?" the man on top of her roared, spit and barbecue sauce flying from his lips.

The next punch obscured Robert's vision, colliding directly in his right eye and immediately turning it dark. But her screams, her horrible, blood-curdling cries, seemed only to egg Paul on. He struck her eye again and again; every time his hand drew back for another blow, it became progressively more red with blood. Soon, it wasn't just blood; there were bits of bone and brain clinging to the hairs on his hand.

Helen's arms went slack. A few more direct blows to that side of her head, and Robert felt himself fading.

Less than a minute later, Robert was transported to the darkness again. Only this time, he wasn't alone.

"Paul," he whispered.

Chapter 33

"DON'T YOU FUCKING DIE on me, Robert!" Carson shouted. "Don't you fucking die!" He quickly moved to Robert's side, and tried to sit him up. His brother was seizing hard, his eyes rolled back in his head, his hands and feet erect and twitching.

"Paul," Robert slurred.

Carson turned to Michael.

"For fuck's sake, help me!"

Michael appeared frozen by the strangeness of the day's events and just stood there, chewing something slowly, deliberately, blood dripping from his lips.

He looked to Bella next.

"Bella? Help me get—"

Robert's body relaxed, and the lack of rigor caused him to slip in Carson's arms. Staring down at his brother, Carson was shocked to see that his eyes were open and he was staring directly at him.

Carson let go completely and stumbled backward, but Robert's hand, the one missing part of a finger, shot out before he could get out of reaching distance. It locked on his throat and windpipe.

Carson grabbed at the hand, desperately trying to peel it away, but Robert's grip was impossibly strong.

Robert sat up and stared him directly in the face. His eyes were dark, bordering on black.

"On the contrary, Paul, I've never felt so alive."

Paul? What the fuck is he talking about?

Carson's eyes darted to Michael, who was still just standing there, gaping like a buffoon. His gaze went to Bella next, but she too seemed frozen in fear, or confusion, or *something*.

His airway was being crushed, and no matter how much he clawed at Robert's hand, it didn't seem to faze him.

"Bella," he tried to say, but the word barely came out more like a croak or a death rattle than an actual word.

Robert started to stand, rising first to a knee, then to his feet. And then he lifted Carson clear off the ground with one hand, his eyes turning completely black. Feet kicking now, Carson could feel his life being squeezed out of him.

And then, just when he felt his consciousness fading, Robert's eyes suddenly went clear, and his hand released Carson.

Coughing, he fell to the ground in a heap, trying to draw a deep breath while massaging his throat.

"Bella," he gasped. "Bella, get him."

That was all he could managed before being overcome by a coughing fit that ended in him spitting a wad of blood onto the floor.

When he looked up, Bella finally animated. She went right to Robert, who was just standing there, a confused expression on his face.

What the fuck just happened?

Robert looked like he hadn't slept in days, and he had several injuries that appeared to predate the beating inflicted by Michael. The wrist that he had held him up by seemed purple, either badly sprained or maybe even broken.

How did he do that? What *did he do?*

Bella kicked Robert in the back of the knee, and he fell hard on his ass and back. He offered no resistance to her even when she pounced on him like a lithe cougar, and started to bind his hands in front of him.

"Robert!" Shelly hollered from Carson's left. In all of the action, he had forgotten that they were even there. Still on his hands and knees, Carson turned his head toward her voice.

The dead, the ones that he was supposed to be in control of, were standing still directly between Shelly's and Cal's cameras.

"Grab them," he croaked, gesturing with his hand to the quiddity. "Grab them. Take them to the Marrow," he repeated in a voice he didn't recognize. But the quiddity didn't move, didn't even fucking twitch.

He had no idea what the hell this camera trick was all about, but whatever it was, it superseded even his orders.

The only quiddity that wasn't standing was the woman with half a face, the one who had sent Allan to the Marrow. But it wasn't just that she lay in a heap on the ground that made her different. For some reason, she just seemed more *real*.

And then, inexplicably, the pile flesh and bone started to move. Just a small twitch at first, but then her entire leg, which had previously been twisted beneath her at an odd angle, started to straighten.

Like a newborn calf, the dead woman started to rise, her one good eye unblinking and aimed directly at Carson.

He swallowed hard.

"Go," he instructed. "Grab the cameras."

But the standing, teetering dead failed to respond to his instructions. Instead, the dead eye flicked over to Robert, who was on his back, hands and feet bound.

"What now, Carson?" Bella asked, her eyes whipping back and forth.

Carson didn't answer right away. He was trying to think, to understand what had happened to Robert, but then shook these thoughts away.

It didn't matter.

What mattered was that they had him now, and he was a Guardian. He could be—he *would* be—used to open the rift.

Leland could deal with all this shit when he came over to this side.

All they needed to do was to bind him between the living and the dead. Problem was, the dead were suddenly camera shy.

Carson looked back at the woman with the hole in her face. She was just standing there, her posture suggesting that she was awaiting instruction.

An instruction that Carson had already delivered.

"Move, goddammit!" he shouted, finally managing to pull himself to his feet.

Again, the woman failed to respond, and Carson threw his arms up in frustration.

When he had envisioned trapping Robert here, in the Harlop Estate where it all began for him, he had pictured things going differently.

Very differently.

But then someone gave an order, and the dead woman finally started to move. Only it wasn't Carson who issued it, but Robert.

Chapter 34

THE WOMAN NAMED HELEN was inside his head. When Robert let go, truly let go, she bubbled to the surface. And only then did the pressure inside his head abate.

In a moment of confusion, he allowed her to take over, to unleash her pent-up fury that was born from her husband's abuse and her murder. Taking a back seat to his own body, Robert watched as Helen grabbed Carson by the throat.

And he almost let her kill him.

But like at Seaforth Prison, it wasn't something that he could bring himself to do—even if he wasn't exactly the orchestrator of his actions.

One kill, as warranted as it was, was enough for Robert.

Like a drowning man clawing at the surface, Robert forced himself to the fore, in the process driving Helen back down into the deep recesses of his mind. For the moment, he was at peace, alone in his own head. But he was also spent, physically and mentally, and was helpless to fight off Bella, who tied him up. When Carson issued the order to the quiddity, however, he felt compelled to act.

With his hands bound, he couldn't control the quiddity as he had before, and in the process allow Cal and Shelly to lower the cameras and get the fuck out of here.

But he could still speak, and for some reason, he thought that he might be able to command the empty sack with the quiddity of Helen now inside him, and that he might exert control over her body.

And if not him, then perhaps Helen would be able to help.

"Grab him," was all he had to say.

The creature strode forward, but the steps were awkward, ratchety, all knees and elbows.

Carson made his way to his feet, and was looking toward Michael and Bella for help.

"What the fuck are you doing? Leland put you in *my* control!" he shouted at Helen's corpse.

Cal, who seemed to have lost his tongue until now, was looking at Robert with a mixture of terror and confusion on his face.

"Robbo, what the fuck is going on? *Robbo!*"

"Grab Carson," Robert demanded again, ignoring his friend. Helen's body took another awkward step.

With every order, he felt resistance, which was strange, given that the contents of her head had been scooped out, and were now inside of his.

As the shirtless, tattooed Michael stepped in front of Carson protectively, Robert turned his thoughts inward.

Helen? Are you there?

Silence.

Helen?

This time, his query was met by a tiny voice.

Where am I?

There was desperation in that small voice. Desperation and fear.

What happened to me?

Robert didn't have the heart to recap her death, or the time to try to explain things that just wouldn't make any sense to her.

"Don't let it come near me," Carson said, a hint of fear on his tongue.

Michael, mouth still dripping blood from where he had bitten off Robert's finger, looked around for something to use as a weapon. He settled on the nearly empty bottle of scotch on the mantle.

Helen, you're safe now. I can explain later, but right now I need your help.

Who are you?

The dead body took another jaunty, lurching step.

"Robbo? What's going on?"

My name is Robert Watts—please, Helen, can you help me?

"Robert?" Shelly asked again.

But Robert closed his eyes and tried to focus.

Helen, I need your help—please, you need to let me move you.

Move me?

Robert took a deep breath. When he had given the commands to the shell, the pressure had returned inside his head. If only he could get Helen to let go, as he had, then he thought might be able to get her body moving again.

Robert was about to open his mouth to say something, to command the creature again, when he felt the pressure in his head subside.

Helen had given him control.

"Get Carson!" he bellowed, and the creature immediately obeyed.

It lunged at Carson, the nails on its hands longer now that the cuticles had been peeled back, a snarl on its rotting mouth.

Michael intercepted her before she got to Carson. He swung the bottle at her, and it cracked against the open hole in her face.

Helen's body staggered, but didn't go down. As Michael tried to retrieve the bottle, which was lodged in the hole that had grown larger upon impact, one of her dirty hands reached up and grabbed his wrist.

"No!" Carson yelled, instinctively pulling back from Michael and Helen, who were but a few paces in front of him.

Robert cringed as well, expecting Michael's eyes to turn black, for both his and Helen's bodies to start to fade.

But that didn't happen. Instead, Helen twisted Michael's arm, using the man's shock and surprise to her advantage. Spinning him around, she drove his wrist up his back until an audible crack filled the room. Michael howled, and Helen gave him a shove and released him.

Robert wasn't completely sure if he had mentally told her to do that, or if Helen had, or if it was acting on its own accord now.

And he wasn't completely sure why Michael hadn't been banished to the Marrow, either.

"Carson? What the hell?" Bella demanded.

"I don't know," Carson replied, taking another cautious step backward. Bella, on the other hand, slipped a blade from somewhere under her black vest and was moving forward.

Carson grabbed her arm, but she shrugged him off. For a second, Robert felt as if he was staring at Shelly's evil doppelganger: determined, stubborn, and tough as nails.

Helen's body didn't bother removing the scotch bottle sticking out of her face. Instead, it strode toward Bella.

Unlike Carson, Bella was undeterred.

They met in the center of the room, Bella's knife whipping through the air with amazing speed.

The first slash cut right through Helen's soot-stained nightgown, making a long, and deep vertical line just above her belly button. Helen's arm reached out, trying to grab either the blade or Bella's wrist, but it was too slow. The second slice cut one of her breasts clean off.

It was an incredibly bizarre scene, not only because of the bottle sticking out of one of the combatants' faces, but that there was no blood at all coming from any of the corpse's wounds.

And yet her mouth was still twisted in a snarl.

Michael made his way to his feet, his right arm hanging limply at his side.

"What the fuck should we do, Carson?"

Bella slashed again and again, effectively flaying the corpse's arms and chest and stomach. But nothing she did seemed to affect Helen's resolve.

She just kept coming.

Eventually, Bella's luck ran out, and one of the corpse's hands entangled in her straight black hair.

There was a tearing sound, and Bella screamed. She was hoisted in the air, but before she could be launched across the room, she reached up and used the knife to slice at her hair.

A huge patch of hair gave way, and Bella dropped to the floor.

Still screaming, she crawled back to Carson and Michael's side.

The dead body stood with its nightgown completely cut away, the pale, nude flesh beneath torn to ribbons, her posture such that she was clearly protecting what was behind her.

And behind her stood Cal and Shelly, their cameras held high, between them the other ten quiddity, still frozen in place.

Robert was on the floor on his back, his feet and hands bound, Jonah's body still steaming just a few feet from where he lay.

And then there was Carson, his face pale, the stupid Cheshire smile for once not plastered on his lips. Michael, blood dripping from his mouth, was breathing heavily, his right arm hanging limply at his side. Bella, her face red, a huge hunk of hair missing on the front of her head, was on his other side.

"Carson?" Bella asked.

They were at a stalemate.

The pressure was increasing inside Robert's head again, and he could sense that her confusion, and her willingness to help, was waning. Without her, he wasn't certain he would be able to control her body, and there was no saying what would happen if he lost her.

Carson looked over at Robert and sneered.

"This ain't over, brother. I'll be back." He started moving toward the door, taking his two accomplices with him. "I'll be back and the rift will be opened, Robert. It was in the prophecy—it *will* be opened, and Dad will return home."

He pointed a long finger at Robert.

"You fucking better believe it."

And then the three of them turned and fled the estate.

Chapter 35

"FUCKING CHRIST, ROBERT! WHAT the fuck just happened?" Shelly demanded, her voice hoarse.

Robert didn't answer right away. The truth was, he was just as confused as Shelly; he had no idea how Helen had ended up in his head, or how he'd managed to order her empty shell of a corpse to do his bidding.

"Robert!" she shouted at him, and he shook his head. He tested the ropes on his hands, and he knew that there was no way he would be able to break free.

Cal spoke up next.

"Robert! A little help here!"

Despite his efforts to get back into shape, Cal had been holding the camera up for the better part of an hour. His entire arm, from the shoulder to his fingertips, was shaking.

Instead of answering, Robert turned his attention inward.

Helen, I need one more thing from you.

And then he thought of the solution to their problem.

The woman's displeasure and discomfort manifested in his mind as a dull throb.

How can I go back, then? How will I ever be able to go back?

Robert thought about this for a moment.

Allan was in the Marrow, as was Amy.

He would get them both back, of that he had no doubt. And when he did, he would take Helen with him.

I'll get you there. I promise. Please, just this one last thing.

There was a pause, and then Robert opened his eyes.

Helen's corpse started to animate again, moving slowly toward Shelly.

"Robert? What's going on, Robert?" Her voice kicked up a notch. "Robert?"

Robert said nothing.

As the corpse approached, it took a lateral step to avoid Shelly.

"Robert?" she nearly whispered.

The corpse moved between the ten other quiddity, taking up residence in the center of their mass, careful not to touch them.

Thank you, Helen. Thank you.

"Put down the camera, Shelly," Robert said softly. "Put down the camera and come to me. You too, Cal."

Shelly's eyes bulged.

"You sure?" she asked.

Robert nodded.

Shelly let out a sigh and she lowered the camera, clearly relieved by the tension release in her arm and shoulder. Cal did the same, and then both of them rushed to him, their eyes fixed on the dead.

The quiddity that had been under Carson's control seemed to hesitate, their eyes lifting slowly, their arms flexing much the way Cal and Shelly had done moments before.

They were confused, the ability to move on their own a surprising turn of events.

One by one, they began to realize that something wasn't right, that there was someone—some*thing*—different among them.

A man with a scar that ran across the front of his forehead turned toward Helen's corpse. There was a moment when Helen tensed, but Robert wasn't sure if it was something he saw, or something he felt in his mind. Either way, it only lasted a second. The man snarled, and then reached over and grabbed Helen by the arm.

The corpse did nothing.

Even when each of the ten other quiddity reached over and grabbed her by the arms, the flaps of skin across her belly, the bottle of whiskey sticking out of her head, she didn't react.

They tore at her with the ferocity of a pack of starving wolves. As they ripped her dead flesh, increasing the magnitude of damage that Bella had dealt by a factor of ten, their eyes started to go black. Their snarls degenerated into one collective wail, and then they all threw their heads back in unison, light spraying from their mouths as if their innards had been replaced by an unimaginable brightness.

Robert shielded his eyes, and he felt Shelly curl up next to him and bury her head in his chest, sobbing.

Somewhere close, Cal was also weeping.

The light grew and grew until it was nearly unbearable to look at. But unlike his friends, Robert persisted.

Just a moment before the massive glowing orb blinked out, Robert saw the silhouette of a young girl, dark amongst the impossibly bright background.

She didn't say anything, didn't even wave. But he knew who it was.

It was Amy.

"I'm coming for you, Amy," he whispered. "I'll do anything to get you back."

Chapter 36

THE CLOAKED ONE HESITATED before taking another step. A shudder passed through his entire being. Taking a deep breath, he closed his eyes.

Screams.

Everyone was screaming.

At least ten, maybe more, quiddity crossing over at the same time.

"Did you feel that?"

Sean looked up at the hooded face, and instinctively fingered the cover of *Inter vivos et mortuos* that lay on the table between them.

He had felt something—something in his stomach and chest, a tightness of sorts.

"Yes," he admitted.

"Is it...is it Robert?"

Sean shrugged.

"I can't tell. Maybe."

"You sure he's okay? You have one of your men with him?"

Sean nodded.

"The best. He'll be fine."

"How long did you tell him to watch Robert for?"

Sean thought about this for a moment before answering.

"I never gave him a timeframe."

"Good, good." The cloaked one's voice was rough, androgynous. A small hand snaked out from beneath the robes and took the book from Sean.

The fingers peeled back the cover, and carefully flipped through the pages until they stopped at a very specific passage.

"A Guardian, bound between worlds, will open the rift," the harsh voice read. Sean knew this passage well. In fact, he knew the entire book nearly by heart. The passage that the cloaked one read now was, in his estimation, was the most important of the entire book.

The Prophecy.

"But the Guardian won't be able to hold it open. Only the quiddity of a child, of a powerful child born of two Guardians, will be able to hold it open and allow souls to pass into the world of the living."

The cloaked one closed the book and shuddered again.

"The worst is yet to come." The voice was harsher than usual. It was so gruff that it grated Sean's nerves. He reached into his pocket and pulled out a cigarette, surprised that his hand was trembling slightly.

"The worst is yet to come, Sean. And we must be prepared for it."

Chapter 37

ALLAN KNOX AWOKE ON a beach. It was a beautiful beach, and although his memory was clouded, he instantly knew where he was.

The Marrow.

As he stared at the waves lapping at the shore, Allan was suddenly struck with a nagging decision that needed to be addressed. It manifested as his own thought, but knowing what he did about the Marrow, he was aware that it was not of his own creation.

He could dive into the Marrow and absolve him of the self, effectively refilling the quality of quiddity for those who have yet to be born.

Allan knew what decision he should make, what decision was right. But he hesitated before making it, his eyes turning upward. The sky had acquired an orange tinge, and it looked as if fire had started to lick at the clouds' fluffy edges.

He *could* give himself to the Marrow, or he could remain whole, unique, an individual, and head into the pregnant fire in the sky.

It was the decision of the *self*, the one that everyone must make on the shore. It was the realization that there was more to this world and others than the selfish desires that guided and often tainted human actions in life.

An error in evolution.

A mistake.

"Before you choose," a voice said, and Allan whipped around. Only he found himself unable to turn, his feet locked in the sand. He looked down and gasped.

The sand was gone; in its place was a thick, black tar. But it was far from inert; there were hands in the muck, holding him in place. Feeling panic start to creep into his chest, Allan tried desperately to lift his foot. He made it a few inches from the surface before another hand reached up and pulled him back down again.

"What's happening?"

A crack of thunder drew his eyes upward again.

The sky erupted into a deep orange inferno that strangely seemed to mirror the blue water beneath. And in this fire, he saw faces—faces that bubbled and popped in and out of existence.

"You have a choice to make," the voice said again. Even though Allan couldn't turn, he knew who was speaking.

Leland Black.

"Guilty as charged. You have a choice to make, Allan, but before you do, consider this: why did you want to find the Marrow in the first place? Because of your parents, correct? No— no, you don't need to answer, just listen. Do you see the irony of your decision? You need to use the very thing—self-aware-ness, a simple glitch in the course of evolution—to decide whether not to give it up. Do you not see the irony here? The circular logic?"

Allan felt a pressing need to make his decision, but Leland's words gave him pause.

"Oh, and one more thing. Ask yourself the following before you drown yourself in the Sea, Allan: what was the point of it all?"

Chapter 38

"BURN THE BASTARD," SHELLY suggested as they stood over Jonah's corpse. "Burn the fucking bastard."

She had since untied Robert, and had been in the process of bandaging up his finger when Cal had asked what they were going to do with the fat man's body.

"Seriously?"

"Well I ain't digging a hole big enough for that slob. Besides, he deserves to be burnt. It's just too bad he's already dead."

Robert watched as Shelly wrapped a piece of gauze over the middle knuckle, where the finger ended.

"Shit, Robert, doesn't it hurt?"

Robert shrugged. It did hurt, but no more or less so than any of his dozen other injuries.

"I'm gonna miss this finger...it was my favorite," Shelly said, clearly trying to lighten the mood. But her voice lacked the proper intonation to be successful.

"Sick," Cal replied.

He held his camera in his hand and was staring at something on the screen.

"Check it out," he said. He stepped over Jonah, and turned the screen so that Shelly and Robert could see.

The first thing Robert saw was Allan lowering the camera and coming to his rescue. He delivered a solid kick, one that none of them had thought the scrawny kid would have been capable of, to Michael's head, and Robert felt a strange sense of pride. But as the scene continued to unfold, the smile melted off his face. The quiddity—*Helen, her name was Helen*—no longer frozen by Allan's camera reached out and grabbed him. His eyes went black, and his entire being started to shake.

Cal panned away, and focused on Robert instead, who was shouting at the top of his lungs. The camera zoomed out, fitting both Robert and Allan, still clutched by the quiddity into the frame.

The image degaussed, and when it returned to normal, the glowing quiddity started to pixelate. As Robert's concentration deepened, the iridescent cubes began to stretch out from the crown of the woman's head like colorful taffy, flowing toward Robert's outstretched hand. As Robert watched his on-screen self's eyes roll back, the colors seemed to be sucked *into him*. The red and yellow and orange hues leaked from Helen's corpse until it had turned completely gray, not unlike Allan's appearance through the red lens.

Robert, on the other hand, was blooming.

And then his eyes turned black and he reached out and grabbed Carson by the throat.

Please, make it stop, Helen begged.

Robert looked away.

"Turn it off," he said. When Cal ignored him, he repeated the demand, this time more forcefully.

He obliged.

"What happened, Robbo? We saw something like this at the cemetery and at Seaforth, but not like *this*. It went…it went *into* you," Cal said softly.

Robert, still looking away, winced when Shelly pushed hard to seal the bandage on his now half-finger.

"Sorry," she grumbled. She too was in obvious shock at what she had seen.

Robert was conflicted. They had seen what he had done, and they could tell that he wasn't right, that something was off.

Cal was right, this wasn't like Seaforth, or even the Seventh Ward.

This was different.

It was different because Helen was in here with him now.

"Robert?" Shelly asked.

"She's...she's in here," he said quietly, pointing at his temple with his nub of a finger. "Somehow...somehow I sucked up her quiddity and now she's in here."

Shelly made a face, and Robert didn't blame her. He knew how he sounded.

He had taken Helen's *self* and combined it with his own.

"What? How?"

Robert shrugged.

"I don't know...I don't know. All I know is that my *self* is now entwined with hers."

Cal squinted at him. Then he rubbed his face and eyes.

"What the fuck, Robert? What does it all mean? Will she ever go to the Marrow?" Cal asked with a sigh.

Robert shrugged.

He couldn't know for certain, but he had promised.

And Helen was quick to remind him of that.

I will get you there one day. Even if I have to find the book again and—

With all that had happened at the estate, Robert had completely forgotten about what had happened at the church.

And about the photo album.

His eyes hardened as he focused on Shelly's face.

"I think there is something that you need to tell me," he said, trying hard to keep his emotions in check.

His anger.

Her image, her round, smiling face staring up at the camera from the church floor, flashed in his mind.

The same church where he had stayed, the part of his life that he couldn't remember.

Shelly just blinked, obviously taken aback by his question.

"You have a secret, and I think it's about time that we bring it all out in the open."

Shelly looked down at her feet, and then opened her mouth to answer. Only, it wasn't her time at the church that she admitted to, but something else.

Something that made Robert's jaw drop.

"Robert, I'm pregnant."

Epilogue

CARSON TRIED TO WRAP his arms around Bella, but she shoved him away.

"How can you be smiling at a time like this?" she demanded, her thin eyebrows knitting. "Seriously, Carson, what the fuck is wrong with you?"

They were back in the basement of Scarsdale Crematorium, and after Carson had searched through the dead bodies and had only counted ten, he couldn't help *but* smile.

Instead of answering, he reached over and hammered the button on the side of the oven. There was an audible click, then the furnace turned on, illuminating his face in a flickering orange and yellow glow.

"Help me with the bodies," he said, turning to Michael. The man's arm was wrapped in a sling made from his shirt, but he was strong, and just one hand would be enough for him to help hoist the bodies into the furnace.

They were of no use to him now…unless…

Michael nodded and stepped forward, but Bella reached out and blocked his path.

"Carson? Seriously? Did you lose your fucking mind in Seaforth? We fucked up—we had our chance, and we lost it. You think that Robert's going to let his guard down now? You think we'll ever get close again?"

When he still didn't answer, she took a deep breath.

"Carson! What the fuck is wrong with you?"

Michael pushed by her, and together they grabbed the first body. With a grunt, and Carson shouldering most of the weight, they put it on the lip before shoving it all the way inside.

Then he took a step backward and watched as the flames started to lick at the underside of the body.

Bella grabbed his arm, and he spun toward her.

"Answer me, Carson."

And then, at long last, he did.

"Because, Bella—because if Robert can do *that*, then so can I."

END

Author's Note

The most frequent question that I get asked as a writer, is *'Where do you get your ideas?'* In a recent video blog on my Facebook page, I explained the inspiration for my first novel, SKIN. The idea for SHALLOW GRAVES was a little bit different; unlike SKIN, it didn't come from an experience, but from an article that I read. It described a man in the UK who was so fed up with funeral costs that when his mother died, he decided to bury her himself, in his own backyard. I was reading a ghost story at the time, so my mindset was such that I asked myself, what if the man's deceased mother was so angry at him for not giving her a proper burial that she came back? And that, dear reader, was the impetus behind the idea that eventually blossomed into Book 1 in the *Haunted Series*. As you well know having read this book, the idea has grown legs and expanded ten-fold; the books in this series all explore a central theme: the illusion of the self and the strange truth that only humans are blessed, or cursed, with self-awareness. I attempt to investigate these ideas, this nihilistic world view of reality, in the context of a good old fashion, good vs. evil, ghost story. Oh, and as you well know, there's a lot of blood... always a lot of blood.

I hope you have enjoyed this adventure so far, and I'm happy to report that it's a long way from over; in fact, Book 5 is available for pre-order now.

So come on, follow me down the rabbit hole. And if you do, and even if you don't, rest assured that it wasn't *you* who made the decision. It was your biology, the three or so pound piece of electric meat behind your eyes that makes you do what you do.

You keep reading and I'll keep writing.
Patrick
January 2017, Montreal